Get Over It

Book One – The Gods Made Me Do It (A spin-off from the Cloverleah Pack series)

By Lisa Oliver

Get Over It (The Gods Made Me Do It #1)

Copyright © Lisa Oliver, 2017

ALL RIGHTS RESERVED

Cover Design by Lisa Oliver

Model – FRANKC_1_193 Courtesy of Paul Henry Serres Photographer (Exclusive license) Copyright Paul Henry Serres.

Model – SC_155 Courtesy of Paul Henry Serres Photographer (Exclusive license) Copyright Paul Henry Serres.

First Edition February 2017

Table of Contents

Dedication

To all my readers: Your support has been so generous over the past month and your excitement at reading about Madison and Sebastian has helped me through some black moments. I do hope I have done these two justice in your eyes. Thank you all from the bottom of my heart.

Phil and Judy – my days would be long, lonely and boring without you. You are both amazing.

Chapter One

Madison Worthington ran his hand over the lapel of his new suit and eyed his reflection critically. The cut was perfect, the dark gray material held a faint sheen under his mirror lights as it emphasized his tight butt and slender waist. Madison patted the trim ends of his golden blond hair where they fell artfully over his face. He kept it short for neatness purposes but he purposefully gave the men in his life something to hold onto on top. He leaned forward and peered at his reflected skin. Eyeliner was expertly applied to bring out a pop in his bright blue eyes. He just needed a spot of lip gloss and he'd be ready to go.

"You're going to knock 'em dead tonight," he said with a smile at his reflection, pushing back familiar negative thoughts about never finding the one meant for him. *If only Damien....* Madison stamped the floor with his elegantly booted foot, shutting down that line of thinking. His days with Damien were well over and his Alpha was happy with Scott. *Mate, I need to find my mate,* he thought, but he shoved that idea away as well. *I have a good life,* he told himself firmly, *I have all I need.*

San Antonio was the biggest gay pack in the country; hell, one of the biggest packs anywhere. His position as Damien's Personal Assistant put him closer to the Alpha than anyone else except Scott and Malacai, the pack second. People trusted him with a myriad of problems, *and I cope with them all.* Madison was proud of his accomplishments and as he gave his reflection one last look, he knew he had every right to be. *I'm far more than the worthless skinny runt my father claimed I was.*

The noise of people yelling hit Madison's ears as he opened his apartment door. This was another reason he loved his position. Damien allowed him to live above the club free of charge. The club was busy, but then it usually was. Rumor had it the Alpha was in town this evening, which probably accounted for the higher than usual volume of noise; although Madison wondered what happened to the music that played twenty-four hours a day. Strutting along the short walkway to the stairs, Madison peered over the balcony and his eyes popped. The place looked like it'd hosted a WWE free-for-all. The sound system was in pieces. There wasn't a solid chair or table left standing and there were even holes in the wall – large, body-sized ones.

"I'm going to be needed in the office," he muttered as he took in the wreckage. He spotted Scott heading in that direction and quickly followed. There was no sign of Damien anywhere.

Scott was talking on the phone when Madison swept into the office the Alpha shared with his mate. The Alpha Mate held up two fingers and Madison tried to curb his impatience. He wanted to know what caused the mess. "Yes, if you could. An estimate would be nice. I can't stress how important it is this is fixed immediately. If you can do it in two days, there will be a hefty bonus for you and the workers. I'll have the manager wait for you. He has my authorization to approve it. Thank you. I'll tell him to expect you first thing in the morning."

Madison shifted his feet. "What happened down there?" He asked as soon as Scott disconnected the call. "It looks as if the entire pack went at it. Why do these things always happen when I'm away?"

"Love the new clothes," Madison preened under Scott's attention. He couldn't help himself. No one else seemed to notice his efforts.

But Scott was nice like that. "Damien and an old friend got reacquainted."

"Reacquainted?" Madison's voice was faint. He'd seen his Alpha in a temper and it wasn't a pretty sight. He was surprised the club was still standing.

"Yep. Reacquainted. Now I need you to..." There was a knock at the office door. "Come in," Scott called.

A *god* stuck his head around the door. There was no other word to describe the height, those muscles, and that face...Madison snapped his mouth shut to stop himself from drooling. "They're still resting peacefully." Oh, and that voice, as beautiful and powerful as the rest of him. Madison couldn't stop staring.

"Good." Scott snapped. "Have a seat. I'm just getting quotes. Sebastian will be paying half."

"Only fair." The gorgeous man turned his attention Madison's way. An embarrassing squeak came out of his mouth as the man said "Hello."

Madison couldn't speak. He could barely get his brain to function. The godlike man smiled and then his right eyebrow quirked in the most delicious fashion. Madison felt light-headed, but for the life of him, he couldn't get his mouth to work.

"Nereus, this is our PA, Madison," Scott said although Madison wasn't paying attention. He was drowning in eyes the color of the sea. "Madison who will be taking my notes. Won't you, Madison? Madison!"

Shit. He had to answer. But all Madison could manage was another squeak. His cheeks burned but he couldn't look away from what could only be described as masculine perfection. He yearned to know how that beard would feel against his skin.

"Madison?" Scott said, "Write!"

Madison managed a nod.

"Maybe it's better if I leave?" the gorgeous one known as Nereus said smoothly. "You can fill me in on the costs and stuff on the way to the Pack House."

Was he going to leave? Before Madison had a chance to...well, Madison wasn't sure what he'd get a chance to do, but the thought of not seeing this man again was crushing. "You aren't staying here?" Wow, his mouth worked.

"Scott invited us to the Pack House. But of course, we'll be here a lot." Oh, that voice, Madison could listen to it all day. His cock was tapping on his buttons and he was worried it would break through.

"Oh good," he managed to say and then flushed again. "I mean how nice."

"If you want, Nereus, why don't you go down to the kitchen and order dinner for us," Scott interrupted. "Order whatever you like."

"Sure." Nereus took Madison's hand and Madison's knees went weak. "It was so nice to meet you, pretty wolf."

Pretty wolf! He likes me. Madison squeaked then cleared his throat. "Yes, I'll look forward to meeting you again. I mean I look forward to meeting with you again. I mean..."

"I understand." Damn it, the laugh was deep and sexy. Madison was ready to strip off his clothes and grab his ankles. "I'll order, Scott. For our rooms?"

"Ours. We have a large table in the apartment. I don't mind replacing it if necessary. The apartment could do with remodeling."

Nereus laughed and left. When the door shut behind him, Madison dropped in a chair. "Oh, my gods..." He said, fanning himself with his hands.

Scot grinned. "Close. Very close."

"What? I mean oh, my! He was... he is... I..." Madison needed to get his brain into gear. He didn't want Scott thinking he was irresponsible but damn, his mind was filled with the god who walked out the door and all the delicious things he wanted to do to him. He could worship that body for hours.

"He's Nereus, son of Poseidon and a friend of Damien's," Scott said with a laugh. "Do not drool on the carpet."

"But he's... he's... I..." Madison was still in shock. His cock was pounding. *Has it been that long since I've been fucked?* Madison reckoned it must have been because all he wanted to do was run after Nereus and plead for a long sticky night between the sheets. Or up a wall...damn, he'd settle for a hand on his dick.

"Look. Let's get this finished and then you can plan how to impress him," Scott said, giving him a pointed look. "We are going to the Pack House but as soon as the contractors are done, we'll be back to inspect."

Inspect. Nereus said he'd be back. And he'd smiled, *at me and called me pretty*. Madison did an internal happy dance and then tried to pull himself together. "Yes! Oh, my gods, yes. I mean of course. We will make sure that everything is finished as fast as possible."

If he had anything to do with it, Madison would have the club fixed and open again within two days. He'd hound the workmen day and night if he had to. His mind half on what Scott was saying, Madison was already planning what outfit would most appeal to the deliciously hunky man who smelled of the sea.

Chapter Two

Sebastian snapped his mouth shut as Scott glared at him across the table. The Alpha Mate might resemble the man who stole his heart, but his temperament was far too modern for Sebastian's taste. He preferred the old days; when men were men and there was none of this shit about having a sensitive side or worse, Sebastian shuddered, manscaping.

"I was simply saying," he said, in defiance of Scott's glare, keen to continue his argument with Damien. That was a man he wouldn't mind having in his bed. Unfortunately, Damien was a top through and through so it would never happen. And now his favorite alpha was mated to someone who clearly didn't have a problem with interrupting what was a perfectly civil conversation.

"Damien knows what you were saying," Scott snapped back, "and if you two had your way, this apartment would be in the same shape as the club was a week ago. Now shut up, the pair of you. I'm going down to the club to make sure everything is back the way it's supposed to be and if my mate has any sense, he'll come too. Personally, after listening to you two bickering like kids for the past week, I don't care if you don't," Scott frowned at Damien who quickly stood, a contrite look on his face. "You two can do what you like."

"I'm coming," Nereus pushed back his chair. "I've got this feeling tonight is going to be a good night." He nudged his cock with his hand and grinned. Sebastian couldn't help but grin back. He and Nereus had been friends for longer than Scott and Damien's lives combined. Maybe he could find someone who could scratch an itch? Sebastian doubted it. The lines between tops and bottoms were clearly defined in Damien's pack. Sebastian needed a big man who could be persuaded to try the receiving end of things and a wolf temperament meant that didn't happen in a pack situation very often. He let Nereus escort Scott out of the apartment and fell in beside Damien.

"You let him talk to you like that all the time?" He hissed at the large alpha. "He's smaller than you and a beta wolf."

"He's my true mate," Damien hissed back with a worried look in Scott's direction as they made their way along a short hallway and started down the stairs to the club. The place was packed. "Believe me, a mate can have your cock in a sling faster than you can say jack shit if he wants to."

"Pff," Sebastian was always ready to argue with his friend. "If you'd..."

He broke off as Nereus froze midstep and then roared, "MATE!" Sebastian could feel the stairs rumble and the sound of rushing water.

Damien leaped forward and grabbed Nereus by the arm, trying to get him to stop. But the sound built like a wave and when Damien grabbed Scott and yelled, "Go damn it, Sebastian, move," he was quick to obey. In his anger, Nereus called the waters and Sebastian knew there'd be hell to pay if Poseidon ever found out.

By the time Sebastian'd reached the top step the club was flooded. Nereus dove off the step he was on, presumably to grab hold of the mate he was yelling about. Sebastian hoped the guy could swim at least. It was going to suck having the son of Poseidon as a mate if the man didn't like water. He watched as big burly Doms grabbed twinks and something to hang onto.

Then his eye caught sight of the last person he expected to see. A bedraggled tiny man, in a mesh top and shorts that barely covered his butt, was fighting the water and losing fast. Sebastian felt the pull immediately, but he resisted.

Don't you dare let your mate drown, his father's words boomed in his head.

He won't, Sebastian was just as capable of arguing with his father as anybody. *He's a shifter. He'll be fine.* But as he watched, Sebastian wasn't so sure. The little man got swept by a wave and there was a lot of debris in the water. Sebastian was aware of Scott fighting with Damien to get to him, but Damien wasn't letting him go. Sebastian scanned the area, hoping one of the other men in the pack would see the little guy's plight. But they were all too busy trying to hang onto anything they could find.

Not even you could be that heartless. Sebastian cursed his father. He wasn't heartless but his heart belonged to someone else. If the drowned waif thought they'd be sharing a Happily Ever After he had a shock coming to him. But Sebastian couldn't let the man drown. He dove off the balcony and swam quickly, grabbing the flailing man under his arms.

"You!" The man stopped wiggling the moment they touched. Bright blue eyes filled with hope and wonder.

Sebastian hated to be a bastard, but he'd had years of practice. "Do you have a room here?" He asked harshly.

The little man nodded, the light in his eyes dimming. "I'm Madison Worthington," he said and then gasped and spluttered as another wave hit him in the face. "I have an apartment upstairs."

Guess I'll be leaving as soon as Nereus gets his shit worked out then, Sebastian thought as he towed Madison back to the stairs. The diminutive shifter couldn't stand and keeping his annoyance to himself, Sebastian swung him up in his arms and strode up the stairs. *I'm just going to see him to his room. That's all,* he told himself firmly. Madison felt perfect in his arms and Sebastian could feel his body respond. *Not happening!*

As soon as Madison opened the door, his room down a long hallway past Damien's apartment, Sebastian set his feet on the floor and took a step back, intending to leave.

"Please don't go," Madison said in a small voice. "I know I look a sight. I'm so sorry. I didn't plan to meet you like this. If you'll just give me twenty minutes I can look good again. That damned water wrecked my hair, and my face, oh my god my face." He ran over to the large mirror that took up most of the wall and gasped, rubbing his hands over streak marks coming from his eyes. "I look a fright; completely bedraggled. All that effort for nothing. My hair and makeup ruined and look at the state of my clothes!" Madison plucked at his top which was translucent thanks to the water. Sebastian forced himself not to notice the slim build and the lightly defined muscles.

"I don't know why you're worried about that stuff," he said gruffly. "Clothes don't make the man and neither does makeup. I can't understand why you wear that rubbish on your face."

Madison's eyes widened, which combined with the black marks had the unfortunate effect of making him look like a raccoon. A cute raccoon but Sebastian wasn't about to be swayed. Nor was he going to take the raccoon into his arms, as much as his body compelled him too.

"I know you think there's a connection between us," he continued when Madison stood dripping on the carpet. "But I'll never take a mate. My heart belongs to someone else and it will stay that way forever."

Madison seemed to crumple for a moment, but then he tilted his chin and his back straightened. Sebastian was impressed despite his ideas. He did know how important mates were to any kind of shifter. "Are you telling me," Madison said in a low voice, "even though you know we're mates, you will never love me? You'll be with me, but won't give me your heart, because it belongs to someone else more worthy of it than me?"

"I'm not going to be with you. You know the man who holds my heart as Alexander the Great. He was a proud warrior, a great man. There will be no other partner for me." Sebastian's heart didn't flinch the way it normally did when he mentioned Alex's name, but he refused to examine why.

"Your heart belongs to a dead man? How the hell am I meant to compete with that?"

Sebastian was more baffled by how Madison was managing to stay upright. The man's body was shaking and once again he forced his feet to stay where they were in case he did something stupid like comfort the little man. Even half-drowned there was something appealing about him. "There is no competition," he said more bluntly than he intended. "Alex holds my heart, wherever he might be. That will never change. I plan to leave here as soon as I can find Nereus and you won't see me again."

"Just like that? You're not even giving me a chance? You don't know anything about me."

"I don't want to know." Sebastian allowed his eyes to roam over Madison's body one last time. It was time to pull on his bastard cape. "Even if I could ever bring myself to find a life partner, it wouldn't be someone like you." He curled his lip up in a sneer even as his insides tore. "You look like you've never handled a weapon in your life. You're not a fighting man. You look more like a butterfly than a wolf shifter. I could never be with someone like you."

Ignoring Madison's gasp, Sebastian strode from the room, slamming the door behind him. If his heart ached at the sound of Madison's sobs, he ignored that too. He needed to find Nereus and get the hell out of San Antonio. Before he did something stupid like hug a crying man.

Chapter Three

Lunchtime the next day found Madison still in bed when he heard a knock at the door. For a moment, he thought it might have been the big man from the night before. How sad was it that he didn't even know his mate's name? But when he heard Raff's soft voice he knew he needed to talk to someone and Raff was a sweet man.

"Hang on," he called out. He quickly dived out of bed and checked his face. He looked like shit, but for the first time since coming to San Antonio, Madison couldn't bring himself to care. He hurried to the door and opened it, shocked to see Nereus holding Raff like he was someone special.

"We're true mates," Raff said quickly and Madison realized his shock was showing. "I hope you don't mind, but we heard about Sebastian and I wanted to know if there was anything we could do to help."

That's the problem with red wolves, Madison thought as he opened the door wider to let them in, *they are just too damned sweet and too cute to kick.* At least he knew his mate's name now, which was something.

"I wanted to apologize for Sebastian. He can be harsh at times," Nereus said softly, as he sat down in a large chair, pulling Raff with him.

"Has he changed his mind about me?"

Nereus quickly dashed that flare of hope with a simple shake of his head. "I haven't spoken to him yet," he said. "I met Raff and...."

Madison knew what that smile was about. While he was lying in his bed alone crying his eyes out, Raff was getting sexed up. *Lucky bastard.* But Madison wasn't about to be bitter about his friend's stroke of luck. He wasn't petty and even through his pain, he recognized Raff needed someone like Nereus in his life.

"Sebastian's not an easy man to deal with," Nereus continued. "He fell in love centuries ago and doesn't seem to be able to let it go. I'm sorry if he came across as mean."

"Yes, with Alexander the Great of all people. He told me," Madison didn't try and hide the bitterness in his voice this time. "Apparently, I don't stack up." He waved his hand, indicating his slim frame, pleased he was wearing his pale blue silk pajamas. Well, he wasn't going to wallow looking like a slob.

"You shouldn't give up on your mate," Raff said urgently. "He has to feel the mating pull the same as you do. It was probably a shock meeting you, that's all."

There was that damn flare of hope again. Madison wanted to grab it with both hands, but he remembered the stern way Sebastian spoke to him; the sneer etched on that smug perfect face. "I don't even see how we can be mates," he said trying to let Raff down gently. "You know we only get one mate in life, and if the great and wonderful Alexander was Sebastian's, then my wolf must be mistaken. It could easily happen. I was in shock at the time."

"Alex wasn't Sebastian's mate. He was just someone Sebastian thought he loved," Nereus said. "There's more, a lot more, but that's his story to tell, not mine. I would suggest you don't give up, though. Mates are special." The smile Nereus had for Raff showed how much he believed that.

Again, with that wretched flare of hope. Madison knew he wasn't mistaken about Sebastian. He was just trying to save face. As soon as their skin touched, his body burned despite being soaked. "He won't talk to me," he said fiddling with the hem of his pajama top. "He said he never planned on seeing me again. He said...." Madison looked over at Nereus. "He said he was going to find you and leave. Why would he need you for that?"

Nereus laughed. "Sebastian can't drive and he'd never attempt to use public transport. He and I teleport everywhere, but he needs me for that. He doesn't have that power of his own."

"So, he's still here?" This time Madison didn't squash his sturdy little hope flame.

"He doesn't have any other way of leaving and I'm not going anywhere." The look Nereus gave Raff was so soft, so full of happiness Madison would have been envious if he had the time.

"Well, what are we sitting around here for?" Madison said jumping up and clapping his hands. "Come on Raff, you have to help me pick out an outfit. I was such a mess last time he saw me. I've got to look my absolute best this time."

Raff didn't look enthusiastic, but Madison put that down to nerves. What sexy little wolf wouldn't be interested in clothes?

/~/~/~/~/

An hour later, looking absolutely immaculate, Madison turned the corner towards Damien's apartment. Damien and Scott were outside their door, talking to Sebastian. *Sebastian, oh my stars, the Fates have been good to me.* Unwilling to interrupt what seemed to be a heated discussion, Madison hung back, his ears straining to hear what was going on. Scott was getting at Sebastian for not wanting to be with him...*oh, no, they're talking about me.* Madison didn't have to strain his ears to hear Sebastian's response. The man yelled loud enough for the whole club to hear.

"I didn't ask for a mate. It's not my fault the Fates fucked up. My true love is dead and has been for centuries. I'm not dishonoring his memory by taking a piddly-assed twink as a mate. My mate will be a warrior; just like my lover was; someone big, capable of looking after himself; instead of worrying about the state of his frigging clothes and water in his hair. The Fates are playing a fucking JOKE on me, and I won't have it. I won't take that twink for a mate if he's the last man on earth."

Hope didn't just die in that instant. It was thoroughly annihilated and Madison was sure he'd die with it. In just a few choice words Sebastian robbed him of any chance of love, happiness or having someone special in his life.

His eyes filling, Madison couldn't help a gasp as his heart broke in two. Scott and Sebastian turned. Unwilling to face the humiliation, Madison ran past them, heading down the stairs. Nereus and Raff were in his apartment and Madison needed to be alone. He headed for the main doors. There were bouncers there and the doors were locked. Madison knew that wasn't right, but he didn't have time to think about it. He was desperate to get out. Away from the pack who'd witnessed his humiliation; away from his mate who'd taken his hopes and dreams and ground them to dust.

He ran to the side entrance. There was never a guard on that door. The lock was stubborn, and Madison pounded at it, determined to get outside.

"Madison, don't go," Scott yelled behind him. "It's not safe...what?" Madison half turned and Scott fell on him, a dart hanging from his neck. As he tumbled to the ground he felt a prick pierce his arm through his suit and then all he knew was darkness.

/~/~/~/~/

"You can't force me to mate your wolf," Sebastian struggled out of the wreckage of Damien's large dining table. The fight with Damien was inevitable. Sebastian would do anything to take away the sight of Madison's stricken face which seemed etched in his memory and as soon as Damien opened his mouth he threw a punch at it.

"No one's forcing anyone," Damien was having similar problems. His leg and arm had gone through the plaster wall. He yanked his foot out, pulling a large chunk of plaster with it. "But you didn't have to be so fucking hurtful. Madison's a sweet man and your words devastated him. He'll never get another mate while you're still breathing and now that his wolf's scented you, he can't be with another partner even if it's just for sex. You're a fucking asshole. You should have left him alone."

"I couldn't let him drown. I'm not a complete bastard." Sebastian brushed off his clothes and looked around for a chair. They were scattered in pieces around the floor. He sat on the kitchen counter instead, resting his head in his hands.

"You could have fooled me," Damien staggered to the kitchen and pulled out a couple of beers. He handed one to Sebastian. "How long has this lover of yours been dead?"

"Two thousand three hundred and thirty-nine years. It will be two thousand three hundred and forty years next June."

Damien's mouth dropped open in shock. "And you haven't been with another man in all that time?"

"Of course, I have," Sebastian took a long swig from the bottle. "Alexander and I weren't mates. But he took my heart with him when he died."

"I also vowed never to love again," Damien said. "You've heard me say that often enough over the years, and then Scott came along and, bam, I couldn't be happier."

"Your mate is strong and of the warrior class. I understand why you mated him. I'd consider it if the twink looked like Scott."

"The twink's name is Madison," Damien snarled and Sebastian realized he'd said the wrong thing again. The Alpha was protective of his PA. "He's older than he looks; has been through a hell of a lot in his life, and then had the misfortune to end up with a mate like you. Now he can't be with anyone else because you're too stuck up to see value in a person beyond his size."

"I'll get the mating broken; I have connections." At least Sebastian hoped those connections still worked. He'd have to go through his father and he and dear old Dad weren't really on speaking terms. "Maybe the Fates will give him another mate."

"And maybe they won't and last I heard no mating could be broken no matter who you were." Damien looked around at the trashed apartment. "Scott is going to have my guts for garters because of this." He frowned and Sebastian knew instantly something was wrong. His gut churned and he was filled with the sensation of dread. To hide it, he focused on his friend.

"D, you okay?"

"Scott... SCOTT!" Flinging his bottle on the floor, Damien ran from the apartment, tugging his shirt off as he went. By the time Sebastian followed him down the stairs, Damien was in wolf form and growling. He ran around to the club's side exit and Sebastian's gut ache worsened as he noticed Madison's shiny black shoe with a note attached. Damien shifted back and grabbed a piece of paper taped to the shoe, snarling as he read it. "Get me a phone."

Sebastian realized in that instant that Madison and Scott were gone. The only thing was, he wasn't sure how he was supposed to feel about it. He didn't want Madison...so why did he feel his life was over?

Chapter Four

Madison groaned and went to rub his head but the clanging of chains stopped him. *Chains? What the fuck? No one's allowed to….* Madison opened his eyes and they widened as he took in his surroundings. "Where the fuck am I?"

His senses were muted. His wolf was there but seemed to be sleeping; but Madison could still pick up the stench of death and blood. He squinted, trying to see in the dim light. The concrete block walls weren't inspiring. Neither was the lack of windows. His cage made Madison's predicament all too real and he spotted torn rags on the floor. His best suit. Madison gulped. He was naked.

Fighting down his terror, Madison hated to be bound in any way, he looked for a way out. His ankles and wrists were shackled, the chains linked to the cage. He could barely straighten his limbs. The cage was set on the floor but the thin blanket covering the bars did little to stop the cold from the concrete seeping through. He whimpered, unable to help himself.

He still wasn't sure where the horrible smell was coming from. It wasn't him; Madison sniffed his armpits to make sure. His phobia about smelling bad and being tied up...*nope, not letting my memories go there*, he thought. *I'm in dire straits as it is.* A perusal of the room wasn't helpful, though. There were racks on the wall filled with the type of things Madison stayed away from at the club. Whips, more chains, knives. Madison shuddered. *Look away from the walls.*

The rest of the view wasn't any better. There were two large steel doors but Madison couldn't see any locks or hinges. There was a large chest in one corner and something...Madison leaned forward, straining his eyes to see. It looked like...Madison scuttled back as far as the chains would let him. It was a body and although Madison wasn't sure, he had a horrible suspicion it was one of the subs from the club. Curling his legs up against his chest, Madison hugged himself, not bothering to hide his fear. He just hoped the fact he couldn't see Scott meant the Alpha Mate hadn't been taken too.

/~/~/~/~/

Madison had no idea how much time passed when one of the doors clanged open and a harsh light shone in the room. A dark-clothed figure strode into the room, a hood half covering his face.

"Oh, don't you look lovely, all pale and scared, wondering what's going to happen to you." The voice was harsh, but Madison knew he'd heard it before. *A pack wolf?* He didn't want to believe it but as the man got closer, his nose told him his captor was definitely a wolf.

"Not got anything to say?" The dark-cloaked man seemed amused. He wandered over to the body and kicked it. "Joel here screamed from the moment he woke up. I thought you'd have more fire, dealing with Damien's demands."

"Will it do me any good?" Madison looked up and tried to see the man's eyes, but of course, they were covered. *Do I know him?*

The man laughed. Not a pleasant sound. "You do have a bit of spirit. I am glad."

"Why am I here? Do I know you? What have I ever done to you?"

"I didn't want you at all," the big man waved his arm at the cage. "I wanted that damn red wolf but he wouldn't leave the club so I had to go with plan B. Ransom. Damien would do anything to get that little blond he's called a mate back."

Scott? Had Scott been taken too? "Where's the Alpha Mate?" Madison was almost afraid to ask, but he had to know. Unfortunately, his kidnapper wasn't obliging because he just laughed.

"I can hardly keep Damien's so-called mate with my toys, now can I? Scott is safe and secure, just like you. I'm hardly going to hurt the man who's going to help me get that red wolf."

That meant Scott was unhurt and if he was okay, then surely his mind link with Damien would have them out of this predicament soon enough. Damien would be scouring the city for his mate. Madison could only hope they'd remember to find him too. Shit, knowing Scott, the Alpha Mate would shift and kill this idiot the first chance he got.

The man rapped on the cage bars and Madison jumped. "Thinking about our heroic Alpha Mate shifting and getting you out of here?" Hell, Madison was already starting to hate that laugh. "Can you feel your little wolf, boy? Is he ready to spring out at me and rip my throat out? I don't think so." The man patted his pocket. "Drugs, boy. Special drugs made to hide scent and stop a shift. Neither you nor the Alpha Mate is going anywhere until I have that red wolf."

"Why is Raff so important to you? Do you know him?" Madison knew Damien wouldn't trade Raff for Scott no matter how much he wanted to.

The man shook his head. "None of your business, boy. Secrets. Alpha secrets. You should be worrying about how you're going to keep me happy. Joel didn't do a very good job and he didn't last long. But then you've been letting the Alpha fuck you for years, so I'm guessing you'll be harder to break."

"I haven't...." Madison snapped his mouth shut. If his captor knew Damien hadn't touched him in over twenty years, then he could become expendable.

"Yes, I know all about him getting rid of his rostered subs when he took that blond into his bed. But he didn't get rid of you, did he? No, I'm thinking you must be something pretty special, spending all that time in the Alpha's office. I can't wait to find out." The man put his hand through the bars, stroking Madison's leg. Madison gritted his teeth although his skin crawled. "Oh yes, so soft. You'll mark beautifully. Here, do you want a sandwich, boy?"

Working to keep his face bland, Madison nodded. The man reached into his coat and pulled out four sandwiches covered in plastic wrap. He reached into another pocket and produced a bottle of water. "You eat and drink, while I attend to other matters and then I'll be back and we'll discuss what you're going to do for me. Don't go away."

Madison took the offerings. He knew he'd be a fool not to. But he wished his wolf wasn't suppressed. He unwrapped and sniffed the sandwiches the moment the man left the room, the clang of the door making him jump. Potted meat. He hated potted meat, but his stomach chose that moment to gurgle so he ate them quickly, trying not to grimace at the taste. The water bottle didn't look tampered with, but the light went out as soon as the door closed. It was darker in the room than before.

"Can't go without water," Madison muttered as he unscrewed the lid. Once he was done, his bladder called to him, but Madison wasn't going to give into those needs unless he had to. The thought of sitting in his own filth was too humiliating for him to handle.

Dizziness hit him and he sank back against the bars. *Damn food must have been drugged, after all,* he thought as he collapsed.

Chapter Five

Sebastian tilted back his head, letting the whiskey run down his throat. It wasn't helping. Nothing helped. He was stuck at the Pack House because Nereus refused to leave his mate's side and what's worse was when he tried to help in the search for Madison and Scott he got yelled at. So what if he said he wouldn't take the man as his mate? He had a right to his opinion. Alexander was everything he ever wanted in a mate. He wasn't going to settle for anyone less.

He tried to conjure up the image of Alexander's face; those proud lines and the curly blond hair that hung to his shoulders. But his mind was filled with a finer face, softer features, full pink lips and a high brow. Bright blue eyes that shone...Sebastian took another swig from the bottle.

"It's not my fault," he yelled at the empty room. The answering silence mocked him. Nereus was staying with Raff; no one wanted to speak to him. He couldn't face Damien; not with the man dying by inches every hour Scott was gone. Sebastian had forgotten about that element of shifter physiology until Nereus bluntly told him to lay off Damien completely.

Unfortunately, deep in his heart of hearts, the one place he was truly honest with himself, Sebastian knew it was his fault. He'd got angry when Scott snarled at him about Madison because he felt guilty. All his father's lectures about mates and their importance had kept him awake all night. He'd managed to block his father eventually, but the words lingered, tormenting him. His only thought, when he'd finally decided to face the world was to leave San Antonio.

If only...a sharp knock at the door stopped that train of thought and Sebastian looked up, his anger surging at the sight of Nereus. The man was so smugly mated it made his teeth clench and he didn't need to deal with his best friend right now.

"I've just about had enough of you," Nereus snarled. Sebastian took a swig from his bottle again, eying his friend silently. "Everyone knows you didn't want Madison as a mate; yet now he's missing you're acting like a love-sick goat whose harem's run off."

"I didn't want to mate him; doesn't mean I wanted anything to happen to him." If Nereus hadn't been so angry, Sebastian might have shared how he felt he'd made a dreadful mistake. But he met anger with like, because that's who he was.

"Well something has happened to him and what are you doing about it? Sitting there getting drunk and acting like an ass."

"Goat. Ass. You are full of colorful terminology today," Sebastian sneered, quaffing more booze. "What's the matter? Why are you even here? Your twink's ass boring you already?" *Gods, I should learn to keep my mouth shut.*

"You've got no right to talk about my mate," Nereus clenched his fists. "Don't think I haven't noticed the way you ignore him every time he's in the room. You're fucking upsetting him and you've got no right. He's kind and sweet and he was willing to sacrifice himself just so Madison and Scott had a chance of coming home. What have you done?"

Of course, I ignore him. He's reminding me of who I'm missing, you ass. Why can't you see that? Sebastian lurched to his feet, his bottle fisted in his hand. "You stopped him from going. This whole mess could've been over by now, but no, your little twink was far too precious to be used as bait."

"You didn't even want your mate. Damien told me; told all of us. You wouldn't mate with Madison if 'he was the last man on earth', so you said. Your poor mate heard you say those very words. I can't imagine how much that must have devastated him. At least I had the guts to accept the decision the Fates made for me."

"Guts. It doesn't take guts to fuck a twink," Sebastian said harshly, his anger putting words into his mouth that should never be spoken between friends. "You've been saddled with a mate; saddled with a worthless twink who'll hang like a leech around your neck for the rest of your existence. Now a warrior on the other hand," Sebastian swung the arm with the bottle attached. "It takes guts to mate a warrior. A real man."

"How would you know?" Nereus seethed. "So you fucked a few thousand of warriors. Whoop-di-do. So have I. And you know what I got out of it? Fucking nothing. Same as you. An itch scratched. That's it."

"Like your twink's any better. I'm surprised you can even get you cock up his ass without him crying."

Nereus closed his eyes and blew out a long breath. "I get love from Raff," he said slowly. "He might not have said the words but I sense it every time he touches me; I feel it every time he welcomes me into his body. That feeling stays with me well after my cock's gone down. He cares about me; cherishes me. Something you know nothing about. He completes me, damn it and I will worship him for the rest of my days."

Sebastian stepped closer, drawn to Nereus's words like a moth to a flame. Gods, how he wanted that in his life. He didn't realize it until Nereus laid it all out, as plain as day, but now he craved it. But Nereus hadn't finished. "I'd rather spend a lifetime of boredom as you call it, being loved by a strong, sweet and wonderful man like my mate than spend five minutes with a toxic mess like you. If you want us to stay friends, then you will treat my mate with the respect he deserves; the same respect I'd give yours if you'd manned up and claimed him."

Sebastian knew his friend was waiting for an answer, but even for him, Nereus's disgusted face was hard to handle. A two-handed shove sent him to the floor, the whiskey spilling all over his clothes. He stared at his friend in shock as the man sneered at him again. "Get your shit together, Sebastian. Wallowing in your own filth isn't doing anybody any favors. Your mate wouldn't want you like this if you begged him on your hands and knees."

Nereus was still shaking his head as he left the room. Sebastian went to stand up, but his head swam and he fell back on the carpet. *What the hell have I done?* But even through the whiskey haze, Sebastian knew what he'd done. His callous words caused two men to be in danger. No one could find them. Well, one man could – his father. But Sebastian didn't know if he dared ask. Surely his father would blame him for this as much as everyone else did?

"Gods, I wish I knew what to do."

/~/~/~/~/

Madison lost track of time. He didn't know if it was day or night. Sometimes his captor would leave the lights on for hours, other times there was nothing but darkness.

The only break in the silence was when the man visited and Madison dreaded those visits. He hadn't been hurt so far. It seemed anticipation was another torture ploy, but Madison knew it was only a matter of time before those words became actions and he dreaded it.

Left alone with his thoughts, Madison thought over his pathetic life. He prayed for death constantly. He stopped eating the food, hoping his wolf would wake up enough for a shift. That didn't work; the man stuck a needle in his arm. Now drugged and dazed all Madison could do was alternate between crying and ranting about the mate who didn't want him.

It was during a crying phase, he thought he heard Scott's voice. Surely not; Scott would have escaped by now. But maybe...? "Scott, is that you? Are you all right?"

"Locked up, but I managed to shift," Scott called back softly. "Got a few options for getting out. How about you?"

"None." Madison tried not to let the fear show in his voice. "There're chains around my ankles and wrists; my wolf's not responding. The cage bars are thick and too close together for me to get through in either form."

"Are there any other doors? Can I get to you?"

"I don't think so. There're two doors but they both look the same. I've seen the asshole use one of those remote key locks which must be how he gets in and out." Madison knew there was no way Scott could break through the doors. They were about four inches thick.

"Is there anything else in there?" Scott said urgently. "Something you can use to get free."

"There's a lot of shit in here, none of it within reach," Madison was losing control. To know Scott was so close, but so far away shattered him. "Believe me, I don't want to be in here any more than Joel obviously did."

"Joel's there with you?"

"Dead."

"Okay." Scott sounded like he was trying to calm his breathing. "Is there any way you can see me getting in there? A window perhaps."

"No. Concrete blocks, two steel doors, a big assed cage, and *manacles*." Madison's voice rose and he tried to stop it, but panic was hitting him hard.

"Is the floor concrete too?"

"Yes! And there're manacles and whips, chains and knives, and some stuff. Fuck, I don't want to see this stuff."

"Madison. You have to calm down, Madison."

"You have to leave and get help," Madison knew it was the only way. "I've got to get out of here. The kidnapper is batshit crazy. He's getting worse. The things he says. He's going to do to me what he did to Joel and you don't want to see the state that poor man is in."

"This is fucking Sebastian's fault," Madison couldn't shut up. His anger, his fear, and fuck he was so tired. "I'm going to go back to the club; I'm going to tell that fucking Sebastian I wouldn't touch him with someone else's dick on a ten-foot pole and I'm going to beat him till he bleeds."

"Okay. I'll get Damien to hold him down for you when it happens. But look, don't do anything stupid, all right? I'll get back as quick as I can."

"I'm stuck in a cage; what kind of stupid can I get up to?" Gods, Scott was usually more onto it than this.

"There's a window in here; my wolf can get through it. I can see daylight. I'll get help." Scott had a window. Praise the Fates.

"You get help ASAP," Madison said quickly. "No fucking Damien when you get back. You get me out first, do you hear me? You promise me you won't do anything but get as many enforcers as you can find and you get your ass back here and get me out. I'm not going to end up like Joel. I'm going to find that arrogant son of a bitch who's supposed to be my mate and I'm going to make him wish he'd never been born... He fucking refused me...."

"I promise. You just keep thinking those positive thoughts; I'll be back before you know it." Madison knew he wasn't thinking positive thoughts, but at least now he had a glimmer of hope. Straining his ears, he heard glass breaking. *Run Scott, fucking run as fast as those legs will carry you. I have got to get out of here before I go mad.*

But it wasn't Madison's lucky day. Within ten minutes of Scott's escape, his captor returned and he wasn't happy. Madison was stuffed into a sack and thrown into the trunk of a car. His spirit broke. There was no way anyone could find him now.

Chapter Six

"What do you mean he wasn't there? Why didn't you get me? How could you leave him? How...how...why...?" Sebastian was going insane. Scott escaped. No one told him. Scott, Damien, and the men from Cloverleah all went to back to find Madison. No one asked him to go. But the kidnapper had already left and taken Madison with him. Now they had no leads and the hopes of Madison being found alive were getting slimmer by the hour.

"There were no scents," Nereus said roughly. "There was nothing but the empty cage Madison had been kept in and Joel's body. For fuck's sake, what did you expect them to do? The enforcers have been scouring the town every fucking minute looking for leads."

"They should have got me," Sebastian said stubbornly. He'd given up on the whiskey, taken a shower and even eaten. He still felt like shit, but some of Nereus's previous words had hit the mark. "I'm a soldier, a warrior, I could have found him."

"No one can find him," Nereus said in a softer tone. "They still don't know who this guy is, although there's a good chance he was pack. But he's not going to be around now he knows Scott can pick out his face."

"He's so little," Sebastian turned towards the window, hugging himself. "He'll be so scared, and what that man plans to do to him. No one deserves that."

"I'll let you know if anyone hears anything. Look, there's something else you should know." The tone of Nereus's voice made Sebastian turn. His friend looked worried and Sebastian felt selfish.

"What is it? Is Raff causing problems?"

"Raff's the best thing that ever happened to me," the sharpness in Nereus's voice returned. "Look, this killer. He believes Raff can get pregnant. Can you believe it? He wants to create a pack of red wolf puppies."

"Raff's not of the god line. Only men like you come from male pregnancies."

Nereus's cheeks flushed. "Regardless, this guy is not going to give up. He wants Raff badly enough to kill for him and I have to think of his safety."

"What can I do?" Sebastian might have acted like an ass but if Nereus and his little mate needed protection then...no, he couldn't. He had to stay here.

Nereus shook his head, waving off his offer anyway. "Damien and the others think Raff would be safer in the Cloverleah pack. There's a good chance the killer wouldn't even consider looking for him there. There are a couple of bears and another wolf coming to adopt Ollie, the little bear cub. When they leave, Raff and I are going back with them."

Sebastian turned towards the window, his thoughts confused. "I can't go," he said, the words falling in a rush. "I know everyone thinks I don't want Madison and to be honest I haven't got a clue where my head is at about the mating side of things. But I can't leave here. Not until I know... one way or the other."

Sebastian felt a strong hand on his shoulder. "I know my friend. I'm glad you want to stay. You will get Madison back and you'll see he'll make the perfect mate for you. Scott and Damien are moving back into town this afternoon. It'll be easier to coordinate the enforcers and search efforts from there. Shall

I tell them you'll meet them after lunch?"

Nodding, Sebastian turned back towards the window, unwilling to watch his friend leave. They weren't joined at the hip, but he and Nereus traveled together for centuries. Now Nereus seemed content to live with a pack, all because of his mate. And as for Sebastian. He didn't know what he was going to do. He just knew he had a mate out there who was trapped and alone with a madman. And it was his fault. Maybe he should call his father...but Sebastian resisted. His father would expect a solemn commitment to mate, and he...gods, he was so confused.

/~/~/~/~/

Madison shivered. He tried to pull the chain loose, his mind slowly unraveling. The chain held fast. He had no fucking luck. His mate hated him. Sebastian-the-bastard would rather fuck Scott. Damien would rather fuck Scott. Everyone.... He stifled a sob. No, that wasn't fair. Scott was Damien's mate. He was the one stuck with a stupid, ungrateful, beautiful, strong, sexy... asshole. Sebastian was an asshole. No questions about it.

Why in fuck's name couldn't he get a single break in his life? Chained like a damn dog to the wall. How many places like this did the guy have? Whatever his captor forced down his throat made him weak and sick. He couldn't smell anymore; his wolf was comatose. If the pack couldn't find his scent, they couldn't trace him. The sob broke through. He tried not to close his eyes; every time he closed his eyes he saw Joel.

The door screeched open and then slammed shut. Madison shivered. *Gods. He's here. Sir. Like I'd call that fucker sir.* And from the slamming of equipment against the concrete walls, Madison guessed his kidnapper was not in a good mood.

"They aren't going to do it. Now the fucking Alpha Mate has escaped, Damien won't budge. I'm not getting that little Red Wolf this way. Which means you're useless to me. Fucking useless."

Madison curled in on himself. He'd spent years putting up with Damien's temper, but this guy was a whole new kind of crazy. A fist in his hair had his head pulled up so Madison was forced to stare crazy in the face. He was sure he knew the man from the club, but he couldn't put a name to the face.

"You're pretty enough," the kidnapper said slowly, licking his lips. Madison felt like a piece of meat. "Yeah, I don't think we have to abandon the plans I have for you. They're never going to find you now and I bet you can scream real loud."

Madison spat at the kidnapper's face; hitting his mark. The next second he found himself slammed against the wall. *Fuck that hurt,* but he still managed to keep the glare on his face. He knew he had no chance now he'd been moved. He could kiss his pack and his life goodbye, but he wasn't going down without a fight.

"Oh, breaking you is going to be fun." The kidnapper's grin was maniacal. "I like fighters. You'll be a lot more fun than the last one. He just begged and cried and screamed. I had to wear ear plugs just to fuck him."

Every instinct told Madison not to take his eyes off the man; even his wolf agreed, and he was half asleep. When the kidnapper left the room, Madison started to relax only to have the door shoved open again; the kidnapping bastard dragging something into the room. It looked like a small cage and Madison's wolf whimpered in his head. The kidnapper sat it upright and attached a rope to it; pulling it into the air. "You'll look real pretty in the coffin."

Gods. Madison kept his mouth shut; refusing to let his whimper escape. He simply stared at the man, terrified as to what he'd do next.

"I have a lot of other goodies." The kidnapper left and then returned, this time dragging a chest. Madison had seen similar chests in the club dungeons.

The kidnapper sauntered over to Madison and he flinched as the man ran his hand over his body. "We are going to have such fun tomorrow." Madison glared at the bastard, refusing to let the man know he'd gotten to him.

"Oh yeah. You are a fighter. It's gonna be real fun. Bet you're a good fuck, too. You would have to be for Damien to keep you as his fuck toy. You are going to make me real happy." The kidnapper laughed as he headed towards the door. "Now don't go anywhere. Anticipation is half the fun. I'll be back when I'm ready and then we can play."

Madison waited until the kidnapper was out of the room before he started to tremble. *Someone get me out of here. Please, gods, Fates, I don't care who. Wherever you are, get me out of here.*

/~/~/~/~/

Sebastian sat in the room Damien had given him above the club. No one had said much on the drive into town. Scott couldn't even look at him and Sebastian wasn't sure if that was because he was suffering from survivor's guilt, or if he still blamed him for the whole mess.

The guilt in Sebastian's gut was growing and he knew instinctively that his m...Madison was in trouble.

I could save him. Sebastian knew that. It was the only thought rattling around in his brain. One call, one favor from his father and Madison would be free. There wasn't anyone in the heavens and earth his father couldn't find. But still, he hesitated. What sort of life could Madison live without a mate?

The light from the bedside lamp caught the jewels in the handle of the dagger he held loosely in his hands. A present from Alexander; the only tangible thing he had left. Over two thousand years old and it still gleamed as it did the day Alexander gave it to him. The memory was bittersweet. It was the day his lover of many years told him they could never be more than friends; as though their long love affair meant nothing.

Alexander had found his soul mate; the twink known as Bagoas.

Sebastian had been ready to tell Alexander everything. Who he was; where he came from. He'd spoken to his father about making Alexander immortal. They would live and rule forever. And then the slimy little cat shifter slinked into camp. One look and Alexander was hooked. Alexander was Bagoas's mate. The knife in Sebastian's hand was the kiss-off gift from the man he loved with everything he was. And then...when he'd tried to break the mating...Sebastian shook his head. He couldn't do it. Even if it meant saving Madison's life, he wouldn't go to the one man who took his Alexander from him. His father would expect him to claim his mate and Sebastian...his gut filled with guilt, his heart heavy...he just wasn't sure he could do it.

Chapter Seven

Hours later Madison was still uselessly tugging on his chains. The cell was dark, only one tiny light offering any relief from the gloom. Although watching the coffin hanging like a warning gave him the shivers. The kidnapper hadn't been back except to drop off some food, muttering about the red wolf the whole time; Madison was thankful for the reprieve he'd been given. Maybe the bastard could keep his anticipation game going long enough to get hit by a passing truck. But who'd save him then? Was anyone even looking for him anymore? Scott escaped what felt like days ago.

Pushing the plate of sandwiches away, the clanging plate was the only relief from the silence. Gods, Madison was sick of fucking potted meat. A tear trickled down his cheek. There was no way he was going to be rescued as long as that asshole kept giving him the scent blockers. He would smell just like a human. Not that it would matter because his mate didn't want him, anyway. No, he couldn't have a nice normal wolf who'd appreciate a pretty twink. He had to get a fucking pain in the ass that was still hung up on a guy from two thousand years ago. Asshole. He sniffled as he rolled onto his side facing the wall.

"Madison."

Great, now he was hearing things. That wasn't the kidnapper's voice and he would have heard that bastard banging open the door. Asshole liked to make an entrance.

"Madison."

He refused to answer.

"*Madison*!" The shout reverberated throughout the room.

Shit. He rolled over and sat up; his wolf immediately recognizing the visitor even if he'd never seen him before. Oh, gods... it was Death. Death had come for him. Death. Thanatos. No more chances to do anything. No chance to find someone who would love him; not like he had anything to hope for that after all he had a mate who didn't want him and... Oh gods... Death.

The chains fell off him. Shit, this was real. It wasn't a dream. All because of that stupid son of a bitch... Well, Madison wasn't going to take Death lying down.

"Fine. Just fucking fine. I don't care." Madison yelled as he threw up his hands, ignoring his naked state. Like Death would care. "It's not like it matters anyway, no one wants me. No one's looking for me. The damn idiot who kidnapped me drags me all over the damn place because of Scott and can't take the time to even grope me, even though he said his full intention is to make me his slave and rape me when he feels like it. But no, he's too fucking busy chasing another man. Throws me in the trunk of his car, drags me off to another location, not because he's keeping me safe; oh no. It's because this other guy is so important to him that he can't get over him after two thousand year... s.... Wait, that's my idiot mate. And let me tell you he is an idiot..."

"I know."

"I put on my best suit; I fixed my hair for him. I take special care of my face, I check for wrinkles every day, well not in here, but what does that asshole tell me? He doesn't do twinks. Like I asked for him? It's what Fate wants you to have because you are the perfect mate for him and come to think of it... it's his fucking fault I'm in here right now because the asshole tells me his heart belongs to another. It was two thousand fucking years ago, cut me a fucking break. But nooooo he just has to ruminate over that loss, like it was my fault they weren't mates. Instead, he makes it plain he doesn't want me, so I had to go running off crying and get Scott and me kidnapped by that weirdo who can't even find time to molest me. Not that I would want him to molest me, but can't someone find some damn time to care about me for a fucking change, instead of running all over the fucking place fussing about men they are never going to get? Noooo. Instead, I end up here, chained to a fucking wall with the same exact fucking problem I had with my damn mate." Madison knew he was rambling but if these were his last moments left breathing, he had things to say.

"I'm your father-in-law."

"So now you show up and that means I'm never going to have a mate because I'm dead, not that they will care. The pervert will just throw my carcass in the river and I'll just float along until someone fishes out my body, if they ever do. Damien will just replace me with a new PA just like he replaced me with a younger prettier sub. My own damn mate will be relieved he can go on pining for some stupid son of a bitch that has been dead longer than any wolf in our pack has been alive. All because the stupid son of a bitch wouldn't let go of some bastard...."

"I'm your father-in-law"

"...who's been dead for centuries! I'm done, I tell you, DONE! I am sick and tired of no one paying any attention to me. I'm a wolf; I have feelings just like they have. I have been rejected so damn many times. And you know what? Frankly, it is their fucking fault. I would have been a good mate for Damien. I know he's found Scott, and that's okay but before he found him. I would have been a very good mate and kept him on track but no... Do you have any idea how hard I worked to make myself useful to the dumb son of a bitch? How hard I worked to make him notice I was more than a sub and then he rewards me by making me a PA and replacing me with another sub, not that it was all bad, but it fucking HURT. He never considered for one moment that I had the possibility of being a mate to him when he didn't even know Scott existed. And God knows the man is so damn disorganized..."

"*I AM YOUR FATHER-IN-LAW.*"

Madison's mouth snapped shut and his eyes widened as Death seemed to grow in stature right before his eyes. Then he fainted.

/~/~/~/~/

The warmth of the bed comforted Madison as he stirred from his sleep. "What a stupid dream."

He sighed and slowly opened his eyes. The room was still dark. It must be very early. Hmm... that meant he'd have enough time to go out to breakfast at that little cafe Scott loved before work. Eggs, bacon, sausage, pancakes and maybe some French toast. He could ogle Brad while he was eating.

"That can be done; although we'd have to leave Brad out of it."

What the fuck? Madison sat up in bed. He blinked as a light came on. Death... well... a very sexy Death, stood in front of him with a tray in his hand. "It wasn't a dream? Am I dead?"

"No, Madison. I wasn't a dream and you're not dead." Thanatos sat the tray on the bed. "Now, what would you like to drink?"

"Coffee."

"Perhaps a Mimosa?"

"Oh yes. If this is being dead, I think I can get used to it."

"You aren't dead, sweetheart. You aren't ever going to die." Thanatos laughed. A tray was settled on the bed with coffee, water and a pitcher of Mimosas on it. As he poured Madison a drink, Thanatos added, "My son is like me, immortal. Since you're his mate, you are also immortal."

"But he hasn't mated me yet." A confused Madison took the drink from him.

"He will."

"Yeah, right." Madison downed the drink and held out the empty glass. "Death... I can't keep calling you Death. What do I call you?"

"Dad? Or Thanatos, but I'd prefer Dad."

"Dad? Dad would work. I haven't called anyone Dad since my father tried to kill me; yelling as he beat me how defective I was as a wolf simply because I'm gay."

"Dad," Thanatos said firmly. "No matter what my idiot son does, you will always be my son. Even if he tries to break the mating bond, I will still consider you my son and you will still be immortal."

"I..." Madison wiped his eyes. "Thank you." *Immortal? I will have to Google what that means exactly.*

"Eat. Then we'll get you back to your home and we will deal with my idiot son who doesn't realize what a treasure he's been given. You will need every ounce of your grit to deal with him. I'm afraid he's the one who'll benefit from this deal if he can get over himself long enough to mate you." Death faded out of sight.

"Damn. I guess I need to get used to that." Madison focused on his food and took a bite. "Oh God. This is so good." Madison wasn't sure how long his good fortune would last, but at least he wasn't eating potted meat. After the time he'd had, he'd take his wins where he could get them.

/~/~/~/~/

Madison took another look in the mirror... mirrors.... *Oh, this was so fantastic*. Every wall in the dressing room reflected his new look. He stroked the jade green silk suit. *Gods, this had to be so expensive*. His fingers traced the buttons on the Eton dress shirt. Never in his lifetime could he have imagined wearing a $45,000 shirt. His reflection smiled. It suited him. It appeared Dea...Dad had wonderful taste.

The room he had been given was full of expensive clothes. Madison touched the tie again. He didn't normally wear ties for the office, but this was the *ultimate* in ties; Diamonds and Gold, a Satya Paul Design Studio tie worth $220,000.

Something Madison had only drooled over in magazines. He didn't even want to contemplate how much money he was wearing. He looked like he was oozing the stuff. And Dad told him to pick out his favorites to wear. Considering his favorite suit was in rags somewhere at the last place he'd been held, Madison was in suit heaven. He took a last look at his reflection for confidence and opened the door.

"You look very nice." Death was sitting in a large armchair, a magazine on his lap.

"I'll get these back to you as soon as I can get changed into my own stuff." Not that Madison was in a hurry to change. The clothes made him feel ten feet tall and yet the boots only had a two-inch heel.

"Why would I want them back? After all, they're yours."

"You mean it?" Madison froze. No one gave away stuff worth that much money. Not in his experience anyway.

"They're yours. Everything in here is yours. It's your room. I filled it with everything I thought you deserved."

"My room?" Damn, he needed to shut his mouth because he was coming across as stupid. Turning slowly Madison took in the deep rich colors; he already knew the feather bed was warm and comfortable. Through a partially opened door, he caught sight of the bathroom containing its own sauna, hot tub, and a rainfall shower head; all of which he'd used and absolutely loved. Madison squeaked, "This is all mine?"

"Of course. You are my son after all."

"Why are you doing this? You don't even know if Sebastian will claim me. I'm fairly sure, after what he said, he won't ever claim me. He wants to get the mating broken." Confused Madison plopped on a chair, looking up at his mate's father.

"You deserve nice things," Death said softly, a small smile gracing his handsome face. "You are my son's mate even if he is an asshole and doesn't accept you, it doesn't change anything. He can't get a mating broken. He doesn't have that power. Madison, I know your life, it's one of my gifts. You're a brave wolf who has fought for everything you have. Damien would've been lucky to have you for a mate until Scott and my son came along. If I want you for my son, even if my other blockhead won't claim you, it's because I know who you are and I'm proud of you. And frankly, I just plain like you."

"I... er... Thank you." Madison didn't know what else to say, so he shut up. Truth be told, he was overwhelmed. No one had ever accepted him so readily before. The fact that it was Death... Madison shook his head.

"You ready to face the pack?"

"Yeah." Madison took the travel bag handed him. "What's this for?"

"In case you want to bring something back. I'll create a shortcut from here to Damien's so you can get to work by opening a door."

"You mean I can stay here, permanently?"

"It's your home now. I wouldn't say you were my son and kick you out the door. Let's go see if my darling son's temperament has been improved by your absence."

Madison closed his eyes for a moment and opened them to Damien's club room.

"Madison!" Scott got to him first and pulled him into a hug. "How did you get away? I was so damn worried. We have been searching everywhere. Thank the Fates you're all right, and just look at you. You look amazing. Who's this with you? Damn, you just appeared out of nowhere. What the fuck?"

There was a chorus of wolves calling his name but Madison's eyes fixed on his mate standing at the back of the room, glowering at his father standing beside him, a casual hand resting on his shoulder. He didn't notice Cody's face paling and Cody fleeing the room. Typically, Sebastian's was the only glare in the room.

Damien came running over, shaking Thanatos's hands. "I don't know who you are, but thank you from the bottom of my heart. Great to see you're back, Madison. You look great. We'll catch up later, I promise, but for now, come on Scott."

"Wait. What?" Scott was wrenched from Madison's hug and thrown over Damien's shoulder. "I kept my promise," he yelled as Damien strode from the room.

Madison felt a shaft of shock as he realized what Scott was talking about. No wonder Damien was in such a hurry. He looked over at where Sebastian had been standing but the man was gone. Seems thing hadn't changed. His mate still didn't want him.

Chapter Eight

"You had no right," Sebastian raged at his father the moment he appeared in the apartment. Of course, his father had come to gloat. "You're not allowed to interfere with the life threads of anyone. If Madison was supposed to be found, he would've been."

"He was supposed to be found, by me apparently." Thanatos clicked his fingers and his favorite chair appeared. He sat and smiled at Sebastian. "The Fates agreed to Madison's rescue. They agreed he's to be immortal. So now he's safe and will live forever."

"They can't do that," Sebastian was shocked. "I haven't made up my mind about him yet. The Fates never interfere in a mortal's life like that. How could they do this to me? That was my gift to give my mate if I chose to claim him."

"You think this is about you?" Thanatos laughed and Sebastian gritted his teeth. "This has got nothing to do with you. This is all about Madison. The one man honed and perfected just for you. His life thread said he was to be immortal and now he is. The Fates were sick and tired of waiting for you to make up your useless mind and start appreciating him for who he is."

"I don't even know him," Sebastian said sulkily. "And I don't want to. I can't see what benefit he'd bring to my life. Now I know he's safe, I'll leave."

"You can do that, yes," Thanatos agreed. "I understand Nereus is in Cloverleah with his sweet mates, but I am sure someone like Lasse or Baby can come and give you a ride to wherever you want to go."

Sebastian frowned. Lasse was an okay guy, but he was always mooning about finding his mate, and Baby...he fucked anything that moved. Which could be fun, at times, but Baby always seemed to get himself into trouble while he was at it. It was a damn nuisance being one of the few godly beings who couldn't freaking translocate himself. "I'll find my own way," he said stiffly. "So, with Madison immortal now, I presume the Fates have broken the mating between us?" He could live without having a mate. He never had problems finding company if he wanted it. But Madison would need the mating broken for his wolf to move on. That would be the best thing for both of them, wouldn't it? But his father had more surprises up his sleeve.

"The Fates decided on this mating and it will stand."

"But that's hardly fair to Madison. He's a wolf shifter. Damien already explained his wolf won't let him be with anyone else now he's scented me. He'll pine...it could kill him...." Sebastian trailed off and his eyes widened.

"That's why the Fates have made him immortal. Madison won't die from this; in fact, he'll be a lot stronger than he ever was. However, you have raised a valid point. After all, you're not a shifter; you could be with anyone you wanted regardless of Madison's existence. That's what you're thinking, isn't it?"

"I'm not that much of an asshole; I won't hook-up with anyone here," Sebastian snapped. He'd had offers in the club, but he couldn't focus on anyone else while Madison was in danger. At least that's what he told himself.

"Well, your hook-up days are over too," Thanatos said and his face was so smug, Sebastian wanted to punch it. But he knew better than to mess with his old man. "The Fates have decided since poor

Madison is cursed with never being able to have sex again, it's only fair you suffer the same way. I'm sure your pride will keep you warm at nights."

The full impact of his father's words hit him like a truck, and Sebastian covered his crotch and then quickly moved his hands away when Thanatos laughed. "Your equipment still works and I'm sure if Madison ever decided to give you the time of day, you'll perform admirably. But he's the only one you'll get hard for again, and just like Madison, the touch from another will make you ill. Consider it a gift from the Fates."

"Huh? Wait. What. Never?" Sebastian wasn't a cock hound, but he loved a tight ass around his dick at least three times a week. More, if he didn't have to work for it. And now.... Sebastian folded his arms across his chest and tilted his chin. "I don't care. There's more to life than sex. I can still travel, fight a good fight and I have friends. I'll be fine."

"I'm so glad to hear it." Thanatos stood and clicked his fingers, sending his chair back to his own home. "You won't have to worry about Madison. He'll be living with me from now on. I'll take care of his needs and ensure he's protected. Have a safe trip, wherever you think you might be going."

Thanatos disappeared and Sebastian looked around the room. It wasn't his home. His earth home was in Greece. He kept an apartment in the Underworld but he couldn't go there or he'd risk running into Madison. Maybe he could call Lasse. But then Lasse was Nereus's brother so he probably knew all about Madison and he didn't want to suffer through a lecture from him.

I'll see if Damien can help me organize a private plane tomorrow, he thought. *I'll go home to Greece and maybe, just maybe Nereus will eventually get tired of Raff and want to meet up again.* Sebastian frowned. *Hang on a minute, Dad said Nereus had mates. More than one. Shit.*

While Sebastian was pleased his friend had his heart's desire, as he sat in the dim light pondering his options, he couldn't deny his heart felt heavy every time he thought of being away from Texas. His last thoughts were that maybe he should stick around for a bit, just to make sure Madison wasn't suffering from any negative after effects from his kidnapping. *Yes, I'll do that. After all, I can head home anytime. I'll just make sure he's okay and then I'll go.*

/~/~/~/~/

"I don't know if I can do this," Madison tugged on the edges of another new jacket, Thanatos watching him with a smile. "You said he was planning to leave. I'll...I know I won't handle it well. I'm having enough trouble with my wolf as it is. Maybe I should just call in sick until he's gone. Damien said I could have as much time off as I need."

"You could do that," Thanatos said, coming over and straightening Madison's tie. "Or you could show your stubborn mate that his presence isn't going to scare you off from doing what you love. You've spent the better part of an hour this morning telling me how much work has piled up since you've been gone. I know you're excited about getting it all straightened out. Don't let Sebastian stop you from enjoying your respected and important position in the pack."

"You just want to come with me and see if you can catch sight of your mate again," Madison grinned. "I wish I knew which sub you spotted. I could arrange a back room for you both."

Thanatos's tanned cheeks turned pink. "I think whoever he is, he's frightened of me," he said. "If I had a name for the face, I would know why."

"Then we'll go to the office and you can look through the pack records," Madison gave up fussing with his clothes. His makeup was flawless, his hair was done in his patented "just been fucked" style and his clothes, thanks to Thanatos were worth more than his weekly wages. He'd never looked so good. "Come on," he said, tugging Thanatos's arm, "let's give one of us a happy ending. If I can't have mine, I'll live vicariously through yours."

Thanatos shuffled his feet and looked down at the leather pants and black shirt he was wearing. "Are you sure I look okay?"

"You look perfect," Madison assured him. "Any one of our young subs would eat you up for breakfast."

"I was rather hoping I could take my special sub out for a meal," Thanatos said, a puzzled look on his face. Madison was still laughing when they went through the portal to the club.

Chapter Nine

Madison hummed as he tapped on his tablet, checking off the things he'd done. The orders were organized, the suppliers paid, Madison sent a strongly worded message to one company who thought they didn't have to pay their drinks tab. Damien didn't mind offering credit, but he expected bills to be paid by the twentieth of the month. Lucius and Vincent were thrilled he was back and even Malacai managed a grunt and a slap on the shoulder when he sauntered into his office.

The phone rang as the door to his office opened. "Madison Worthington, how may I help you?" He said, his eyes widening as Sebastian's head appeared around the door.

"Damien's not available at the moment," he said into the phone, trying to maintain his professionalism as Sebastian's scent hit his nose and headed straight down to his cock. "If you are interested in booking a function, I can put you through to the restaurant."

"Uh huh."

"Uh huh."

"I'm sure that won't be a problem." Madison forcibly lowered his voice from a threatened squeak as Sebastian sat in the chair right in front of him. "If you get a confirmation on the numbers by Friday at the latest, I will see to it the restaurant holds your table. Was there anything else I can help you with today?"

Madison hoped the client on the other end was one who would spend the next fifteen minutes worried about menu choices and table decorations. But it wasn't to be. The client was a regular who often held meetings in the restaurant or a private room. With a pleasant goodbye, the call ended.

"Can I help you?" Madison inquired in his best, 'I might know you but I don't have to like you' tone he used for some of the snotty pack Doms who thought they could boss him around. Sebastian was looking gorgeous. Tall, muscled. Grumpy. *Just my type,* Madison sighed to himself as he made a point of meeting those stern gray eyes.

"I came to see if you were feeling all right. I was surprised to hear you were back at work so soon."

Damn it. He has the voice as well; low, husky with a hint of authority. "I don't see it's any concern of yours, but I'm perfectly fine, thank you," Madison said pertly. He knew how to be polite. "Now, was there anything else? As you can see I am terribly busy?"

"I just wanted to be sure you hadn't suffered any ill-effects from your recent kidnapping."

"Oh, I see." And Madison did see. Sebastian thought he was weak and knowing that gave Madison's anger the push it needed to come out. "Well, let me assure you that it will take more than a spineless wimp who had to keep me chained, naked and drugged to bring me down. Hell, I just described my childhood. What a laugh. Believe me; nothing happened that was any different to what I've been through before. So, you can take any fake concern you might have and shove it."

"You were drugged and chained as a child?" Sebastian got this gorgeous little furrow between his eyes when he was frowning. Not that Madison would admit to noticing.

"Are we going to sit here and discuss childhoods now?" Madison snapped. "Since when it is any business of yours? You rejected me, remember; told me you wouldn't mate me even if I was the last man on earth."

Sebastian opened his mouth to answer and Madison stood up. He might not be tall, but he'd take any advantage he could get.

"I don't give a shit about your fake concern, or your sudden compulsion to learn anything about me. You're clinging to the memory of a two-thousand-year-old dead man and you call that love. It's pathetic but hey, good luck to you. I don't need you. I don't need you coming in to check on me. I didn't ask you to love me and I wouldn't ask you to mate with me if *you* were the last man on earth. I am Madison Worthington. I am a wolf shifter and I have an important position in the largest pack in the United States. I could click my fingers and a dozen men out in that club would come running to keep me company. I don't need you."

Madison swept his tablet off the desk and moved passed Sebastian heading for the door. "Now, if you don't mind, I have an important engagement. If you need help with plane reservations or anything, leave a note on my desk. After all, there's no reason for you to stay here anymore, is there; Dad's already told me you planned to leave at the earliest opportunity. It can't come soon enough for me."

Yes, made it to the door. Don't slam it. Don't trip. Madison gave a fist pump as the door made an effective barrier between him and his mate. His wolf howled and cried in his head, but he was determined to ignore his animal half. Just the same as he could ignore a weeping cock and the tears in his eyes. Every cell in his body ached to run back and jump into Sebastian's lap and beg for anything the man would give him.

But Madison would not debase himself. Nor would he do anything stupid. He'd done that too often in his life. Straightening his spine, he walked down the corridor with his head held high, his fancy boots making a satisfying click on the wooden floor.

/~/~/~/~/

Sebastian shook his head, marveling at the difference between the timid, almost childish man he'd saved from the flood and the man who strutted out of the office like he owned the world. "He yelled at me," he muttered. There weren't many people who'd have the balls to do that. Sebastian carried an edge about him his whole life. But it didn't seem to bother the pretty one the Fates thought perfect for him.

"Hmm, what to do?" He tapped his lip thoughtfully. If he had any common sense, he'd leave his details on Madison's desk and get the first plane to Europe. But Sebastian was intrigued. Madison was different than his first impression. A lot different and Sebastian wanted to know more.

Madison's assertions that he didn't want to mate, Sebastian dismissed immediately. Madison was angry and he had every right to be. Sebastian could admit he'd been an ass when he had to. *This could be one of those times,* he thought with a grin.

"Dinner," he decided. "A nice dinner date. Surely, Madison can't turn me down for that."

Rummaging around on Madison's desk, Sebastian found a pen and paper and quickly wrote a note before hurrying from the room. Heading down to the club he saw a small sub, serving drinks. The man's eyes just about popped out when Sebastian stood in front of him.

"Do you know where Madison is?" He asked brusquely, forcing the man to look up at him, instead of down at the bulge in his pants.

"He's with the scary one," the sub said quietly, unable to hold eye contact. "The man who saved him; they're in the bosses' office."

Sebastian thought for a second and then slipped his hand into his pocket, pulling out a hundred dollar bill. He thought the sub's eyes were going to pop out of his head. "Take this message to him, please. Make sure you hand it to him personally. This is for your trouble."

"I'm a house sub, sir. You don't have to pay me. I'm available to do whatever you require."

"I require you to take this message to Madison and to take the tip for your trouble. I don't require anything else."

"You're wasting your time with Madison," the young man said in a snit. "He doesn't put out for anyone. He thinks he's too good for the likes of us since he started working for the boss. Seems to forget he was on Damien's roster once, just like the rest of us were until Scott came along."

Sebastian filed away that piece of information and sent the man on his way. As he wandered over to the restaurant to make his reservation, he couldn't help but think how hard life must have been for Madison if he'd been a rostered sub. Had anyone bothered to care for the man before? Lost in thought, Sebastian retired to his room and lay on the bed, staring at the ceiling. The more he thought about it, the more he realized there was a lot more to Madison than perfectly applied eyeliner and

lips accentuated by products. He
found he liked that idea.

Chapter Ten

Madison was showing Thanatos how to use the pack database when there was a knock at the office door.

"Come in," he called out, pointing at the screen. "If you click here, you get all of the photos in a gallery format. See?"

The door opened and he looked up. It was Toby one of the house subs. "Yes, Toby, is everything all right?"

"It's all right with me," the saucy man sauntered over to the desk. "Some big guy just gave me a hundred bucks and all I had to do was pass you this note. I think I'll go and get my hair cut and buy some new clothes. Then I can be ready to comfort that sexy hunk when you turn him down. I wouldn't kick him out of my bed."

"You wouldn't kick anyone out of your bed, Toby. Some of us have standards." Madison took the note and scanned the contents with a sigh. He looked up to see Thanatos and Toby looking at him. "The gallery, right. Now just scroll down here and all the subs are listed," he said to Thanatos. Turning to Toby, he said, "No reply necessary and I'd save your tip if I was you. Sebastian will be dining with me tonight, and if you want a permanent master it might pay to stop thinking with your dick and start thinking what else you have to offer."

"Why should you get first dibs on all the new visitors?" Toby pouted. "Everyone knows you're frigid. Why don't you let Sebastian go out with someone who'll actually put out for a change?"

"I'm sure if he wanted you, he would have asked you," Madison said firmly, ignoring the frigid comment. "Now, some of us have work to do and a date to prepare for. Piss off."

"I'll get him," Toby mumbled as he left the office. "Fucking frigid pants won't keep a man for long."

Madison let out a long breath as the door slammed behind the bitter young man. "I'm sorry you had to hear that," he said to Thanatos who had a small smile on his face.

"Don't worry about it," Thanatos said kindly. "I've been called a lot worse in my time and there's nothing wrong with being picky. I'm more curious why my son sent you a dinner invitation?"

"You're not the only one," Madison said, picking up his tablet and entering the dinner date for seven pm that evening. "I yelled at him this morning and told him I didn't want him as a mate. I didn't mean it of course, but he...."

"You don't have to explain." Thanatos laughed. "And if I were you, I'd hang onto your temper for a while. That son of mine has never chased anyone in his life. It won't do him any harm."

"Yes, well, I will worry about why he's doing this later. How are you getting on with those files?"

Thanatos looked at the screen and scrolled down the page, his eyes scanning quickly. "There," he said, pointing at a picture of a blond with bright blue eyes. "That's the man whose soul called to me the moment I saw him leaving the club when I took you back."

"Cody," Madison said, biting his lip. "He hasn't had an easy time of things."

"He wasn't born with that name?"

Madison shook his head, tapping the screen on his tablet, checking his files. "He never told us his real name. A man named Jacob introduced him to the club and the pack, told Damien he'd been wandering the streets, but that he was a trained sub. Damien took him in, and over time he worked his way onto Damien's sub roster. We found out later Jacob abducted him from his family when he was still a child and abused him until he learned to be an excellently trained sub. Jacob threatened to kill him and his family members if he ever revealed the truth. We didn't know any of this at the time, of course," he added quickly when Thanatos's face showed his horror. "None of this came out until after Damien took Scott as a mate. The subs were released from the roster and...there was a fire at the pack grounds. Scott saved seven other young boys that day."

"What about Cody?"

"When Damien found out Cody was one of Jacob's previous efforts at training the perfect alpha mate, he offered him a permanent home at the pack house if he wanted it. Gave him a cash settlement, said he could go to college, do whatever he wanted and Damien would support him. Damien was gutted, as you can imagine. He wanted Cody to go to a therapist, but Cody refused. Said he liked his life and that his parents probably thought he was dead. They were old school and didn't believe in gay wolves apparently, so he said he was happy enough staying where he was."

"What a tragically hard life," Thanatos said quietly. "That poor young man."

"He won't want your pity," Madison warned. He'd always counted Cody as one of his few friends. "Yes, he's had a rough childhood and grown up quicker than most, but he's a really nice person, a kind man, and he'd make a lovely mate. Don't go thinking he's not worth anything because he's worth ten of most of the subs around here."

"I think he needs someone to look after him and keep him safe; show him what love truly is; and keep showing him that every day," Thanatos said gravely, and then he grinned. "What? You think I'm going to turn down the chance of a true mate simply because he's had a rough past? I've seen the worst, the very worst that souls can do to each other. It sickens me to my core sometimes, but I have my responsibilities and I can't shirk them, no matter what I feel. But it doesn't mean I don't want someone loving and warm to come home to at the end of a rough day. Even godly beings need a hug sometimes."

"I know Cody could do with one," Madison said. "Joel, one of our other subs, was killed by the guy who kidnapped me and Scott. He was Cody's closest friend and another one who'd been abducted as a child."

"That was really tragic," Thanatos shook his head. "Unfortunately,

Joel's time was meant to end that way. The Fates promised me that he'd be reborn, though, in a far happier situation this time."

"You talk to them?" Madison always believed the Fates were mythical beings who existed in some ether somewhere.

"Who do you think gives me my instructions?" Thanatos smiled. "There are some deaths that can be avoided; the Fates ask me to intervene in those cases. There are other times when death might be inevitable and yet the Fates feel those people need some comfort during their passing. I am there for all those situations."

"Why did you come for me? Was it because of this tenuous tie with Sebastian?" Madison wondered about that. He wasn't anyone special to the Fates or anyone else for that matter.

"The Fates knew you were special from the moment you were born. Sebastian..." Thanatos sighed. "He could have done a lot of damage with this Alexander business if things had gone his way. Alexander did a lot of good for the world as it was then, but when it came down it, he was born human and was meant to stay that way. Sebastian still hasn't forgiven me for interfering, but the Fates weren't going to let you suffer because of his stupidity. Despite his age, my son still has a lot of growing up to do."

"I'm not sure this dinner is a good idea," Madison confessed quietly, fiddling with his tablet.

"I think it's a perfect idea," Thanatos said. "Now come on, if your work is finished for the day, I want you to take me to Cody's room. I doubt he will be there, but once I have his essence, I will be able to find him. Then you can go and get ready for your date."

"And you will track down your mate." Madison leaned over and gave Thanatos a hug which surprised them both. "You are a good man. Don't let Cody send you away. You need each other."

"And Sebastian needs you," Thanatos said warmly. "Don't ever doubt it and don't ever doubt your worth. You'll be the making of my son, I have no doubts."

"Well, that's one of us," Madison mumbled as he took his new friend, his new dad, through the club to track down his missing mate. He had roughly two hours to freak out over what he was going to wear for his dinner date and he'd need every minute of it. *What was Sebastian playing at?*

Chapter Eleven

Sebastian was just toweling off from the shower when he realized he wasn't alone. "What the hell do you want?" he said dropping his towel and sauntering over to his dresser.

"I came to see if you needed comforting, or someone to knock some sense into you, seeing as you've done what no other beings have ever contemplated doing in their life." Lasse, Nereus's brother lounged against the bed, a smirk on his handsome face. He looked a lot like his brother; only his lighter hair and beard and a stronger face differentiated the two. Like Nereus, he was six foot seven, muscles built on muscles and a laid-back attitude. Sebastian didn't need to ask what he was talking about.

"Whatever happens between me and Madison is no concern of yours, your brothers or your father," he said firmly as he pulled pants out of the dresser and stepped into them. "You Mers spend far too much time gossiping."

"But this is delicious news," Lasse beamed. "First Nereus, then Abraxas and now you. The Fates are finally smiling on us."

A snarky comment tickled the end of his tongue, but Sebastian swallowed it. Hard man he might be, but Lasse was like Nereus in one other aspect. They both wanted to find their mates and had spent a hundred dozen lifetimes looking.

"I had a very specific mate in mind if I ever thought of one at all," he said in a gentler voice than he might have used. "Madison is nothing like I expected and I don't know if I can claim him. He's very different than who I'm used to."

"Then let me meet him," Lasse teased. "I'm sure if he and I hit it off, I can get Dad to put in a good word with the Fates for me. Then you'd be off the hook and can go back to pining for the beloved Alexander."

Sebastian had Lasse up against the wall in an instant, his forearm pressing on Lasse's throat. "You stay away from Madison and don't talk about Alexander. Neither one of them has anything to do with you," he growled.

"Pff," Lasse shook him off easily, flicking back his hair. "You can't have it both ways, cousin. If you buried your heart with the illustrious Alexander, then how is it fair to play with Madison's affections? Word has it, you can't stand him because he's a twink."

"Gods, you guys are too much sometimes," Sebastian pulled a shirt from the closet and slipped it over his shoulders. "I was shocked, okay? Nereus flooded the club because his mate was being manhandled. Madison was drowning. It wasn't an ideal meeting. All he could grumble about was his freaking hair and makeup. What kind of man does that?"

"Someone who doesn't have a lot of self-confidence and who prides himself on looking good so people won't mock him, perhaps?" Lasse tilted his head in a move that so was like his brother it was uncanny.

Sebastian frowned. "You think it's a confidence issue? I swear, if you'd heard him yelling at me earlier you wouldn't think he had a problem with anyone."

"He yelled at you? That's wonderful. It means he cares enough to be angry at you." Lasse clapped his hands.

Shaking his head, Sebastian threaded his belt through his belt loops. The grim reaper belt buckle had been a gag gift from Nereus. "He told me he didn't want to mate with me and even offered to arrange my plane ride back to Greece," he said with a chuckle.

"And you're intrigued by that," Lasse grinned. "He's not falling at your feet begging for a lick of your cock."

"Not yet, no." Sebastian checked his hair and gave his reflection an approving nod. "But the night is young. You're not the only one who knows how to be charming. Now piss off. I don't want to be late."

"I'd get my boots under that bed pretty quick if I were you," Lasse said as a parting shot. "Dad's seen your man in the water and he likes what he sees."

"Piss off," Sebastian yelled as Lasse disappeared. *Fucking Poseidon, that's all I need. Guy can't keep his pants zipped for five minutes.* Checking he had his wallet, suitable cash and his boots were unmarked, Sebastian strode out of the apartment, determined to be his most charming. How hard could it be?

/~/~/~/~/

Madison was having fun. The meal was lovely, he knew his suit looked divine on him and Sebastian was clearly trying to be more than strong, silent and surly. But none of that was the cause of his amusement. He realized as he delicately munched on the wonderfully stuffed mushrooms the chef cooked especially for him, that he hadn't dated anyone at the club in...years. And while he should be focusing on his date for the evening, he was getting a wonderful amount of attention from a lot of the unattached Doms in the club.

He smiled as Rob, a sweet house sub brought him yet another drink. "From Peter," Rob whispered, casting a worried look at Sebastian. "He wants to know if you'd have a late supper with him."

Madison's mouth twitched as he placed the glass with the other five already littering the table. "I'm not sure what I'm doing later," he said quietly. "But send him my thanks and let him know I will message him tomorrow."

Rob winked and sauntered off, presumably to deliver the message. "Do you have to keep doing that?" Sebastian grumbled.

"Doing what?" Madison smiled innocently. His youthful face was good for something.

"Six men sent you cocktails this evening, and you've promised to message each one of them tomorrow." Sebastian stabbed his lamb chop as though it'd insulted him.

"It's the polite thing to do," Madison said sweetly, picking up another small forkful of mushroom. He did not want to slop his food on his beautiful tie. "Now, you were telling me about...the crusade campaigns in Europe I believe. You and your friend were fighting I think you said. Carry on. It's fascinating."

"Actually," Sebastian laid down his fork, his lips twitching slightly as he rested his elbows on the table. "Tell me about shifting, what it's like to be a wolf shifter? Is it hard to control your animal side, or is it something you just know instinctively?"

"Oh." For a moment, Madison was flustered. He'd lived with shifters all his life. He'd never had to explain his wolf side. "My wolf is me. Through him, I have increased senses of smell, taste, sight and hearing. I've never really been without him so I don't quite know what it is you're asking. If you're worried I might suddenly turn furry and bite you, that's not going to happen." His wolf wanted nothing more than to bite the hunk in front of him, but Madison was determined it wasn't going to happen.

"Not even when your body's writhing beneath mine and your cock is begging to climax?" Sebastian leaned forward, his voice a sultry whisper.

Oh shit, I need to get out of here, Madison thought in a panic. Sebastian's scent had been overwhelming him for hours. One touch and he'd ruin his suit pants. He carefully placed his napkin on the table and managed to smile. "It's not anything you're likely to find out, is it? Given how you've refused to claim me. I'm not the type to have casual sex with a man who's meant to be mine."

He stood up, using his tablet to hide the lump in his pants. "Thank you for a lovely evening. It was a delicious meal and I truly enjoyed hearing about your exploits throughout history. I've always thought history was a fascinating topic. Now if you will excuse me, I have a lot of work to do tomorrow and messages to return."

He turned to leave, but Sebastian's voice stopped him. "Are you running away from me, Madison?"

"Running away?" Madison turned back to the table. "You have the nerve to accuse me of running away when the whole pack knows you don't want me because of what I look like? That you rejected our mating so loudly the men in Cloverleah probably heard you? There are a dozen men here who'd fall for what you call charm; your stories of blood and gore and how many narrow escapes you've had in wartime. The only time you wanted to talk about me was when your mind hit the gutter. Well, it can stay there, but I won't be joining you. The next time I'm in bed with another person it will be someone who's bothered to learn a bit about me first."

"You can't!" Sebastian's glower deepened. "Your wolf won't let you be with anyone else."

"I'm one of the best bottoms around, mate and I have nerves of steel. I can do what I fucking like." Cheeks flushing as a round of applause came from the surrounding tables; Madison forced himself not to run as he turned his back on Sebastian and made his way to his office where Thanatos installed a permanent portal. It wasn't until he was in the privacy of his bedroom that he allowed his wolf free and his lonely howl rang through the underworld. *At least no one in the pack can hear me.*

/~/~/~/~/

Sebastian sat at the table long after Madison had gone, draining first his glass, then starting in on the drinks left for Madison. No amount of cocktails or fruit juice would quell the jealousy burning in his gut. His dad had told him Madison would get sick if anyone else touched him, *but maybe that's only after he's been claimed.* As a bottom, if Madison was keen enough, he could be on the receiving end, if he could do it without throwing up. Sebastian didn't think that was a kink many people shared.

What he needed to do was talk to another shifter, but Damien and Scott were at the pack house twenty minutes' drive away and he really didn't know any of the others well enough to talk about his sex life. *I really need to learn to drive,* he thought. And then he smiled as another idea hit him. Unwilling to let any of the eager ears around him listen in on his conversation, he waited until he was in his room before he pulled out his phone.

"Nereus buddy, I hear you have two mates now. Lucky bastard. Congratulations. Hey, can you ask Raff if he knows if Madison can drive a car?"

"Yes, I know I should have learned decades ago...yes, I am trying to find a way to spend more time with my mate...no, he doesn't want me, he's made that perfectly clear." Sebastian listened for a moment and then nodded. "Thanks. Will do. Later." Hanging up, he clicked his fingers and the laptop from his old room in the Underworld appeared.

"Change the internet settings, there we go. Hello, Google. I want to buy a car. San Antonio, Texas."

Chuckling to himself, Sebastian scrolled through the listings looking for something that would appeal to his feisty mate. Yes, he was getting more comfortable with the mate word. In fact, the more times Madison yelled at him, the happier he got. "Hmm, red, I think, and definitely a convertible," he muttered happily as he saw the ideal vehicle.

Chapter Twelve

Madison was going over the stock records with John, the bar manager when Malacai and Elijah turned up. Malacai was looking as stoic as he always did but Elijah's face was the picture of excitement. It was surprising to the see the doctor away from pack grounds during the day, but Madison didn't think about it too much. Malacai checked in every day and it was likely he wanted Elijah with him. The couple was sweet like that.

"Hey guys," Madison greeted them and went back to his stock records. He looked at the space where four bottles of whisky should have been. There was only one. Theft wasn't rife in the club, but it happened on occasion. Usually if a visiting shifter or human managed to get behind the bar. None of the pack members were stupid enough to steal from Damien.

Madison caught Elijah fidgeting out of the corner of his eye. "Were you looking for me specifically?"

"Yes," Elijah burst out. "You have to come and see. It's big and shiny and such a lovely shade of red."

"What is?" Madison looked at Malacai, his eyebrows raised.

"There's a delivery out front for Madison Worthington. I think you have an admirer."

"Well, get them to bring it inside." Madison went back to his tablet or he tried to. Malacai plucked it out of his hands, gave it to John and taking him by the elbow, said, "Come on. The delivery guy needs you to sign for it."

"Sign for what?" Madison looked longingly at his tablet, but Malacai was impossible to resist. Madison huffed in protest but he allowed himself to be towed along. He wasn't about to tell the pack second that he needed to keep working or he'd be huddled in bed surrounded by damp tissues. He hadn't heard from Sebastian all morning, and his heart hurt, despite his brave words the night before.

The sunlight was bright, although the air was crisp. Madison looked up and down the road. "What am I looking at?"

"This." Elijah dragged him across the footpath and almost shoved his face in the paintwork of a bright red convertible. "It's yours. Greg here is waiting to sign over the paperwork."

"Mine?" Madison turned to see an older man in overalls holding out a clipboard. He quickly scanned the papers. The car was his. Insurance paid. Warranty. Everything was fully paid for. Madison peered at the payer's details. Sebastian D'Eath. *Very funny.*

"Well, are you going to sign for the damn thing or not?" Overall guy, or Greg as Elijah called him, clearly wasn't blessed with patience. Madison cast a look at the car. He didn't have a clue about vehicles. The car had a pretty emblem on the end of the long hood. The interior was cream leather and it was a two-seater, not a four. Madison could see himself behind the wheel. A gift from Sebastian was bound to come with strings, but it was so pretty.

"Oh, stuff it," he said crossly, signing the dotted line at the bottom of the page. "It's definitely mine, correct? No co-ownership or anything stupid?"

"All yours, buddy." Greg threw him the keys. "Heated seats, remote key locking, automatic engine start for cold mornings, the window defroster is brand new and it's been fully serviced and comes with a full tank of gas."

"Damn, how much would something like this cost?" Elijah was touching the hood carefully, his eyes falling out of his head.

"It's one of a kind, brand new." Greg named a high five-figure sum and Elijah squeaked. Madison felt like doing the same thing, but he was distracted by the softness of the leather upholstery. He was a sucker for leather especially when it still had that distinctive smell.

"Can I come for your test drive, can I, can I?" Elijah was bouncing he was so excited. "I've never seen anything so pretty before."

Madison looked over at Malacai who was shaking his head at his mate's antics. The car wouldn't take three people. "An hour," Malacai said sternly. "One hour and stick to main roads. No funny business."

Elijah bounced over to Malacai, gave him a quick kiss on the cheek and was in the car before Madison could blink. "Come on Madison; let's see how fast this baby can go."

Madison felt a fissure of excitement. He'd been driving for years, but always used the pack vehicles when he had to go anywhere. Stodgy black SUVs couldn't compare to a tricked out convertible. He started the engine, which gave a low rumble and grinned at Elijah. "Put your seat belt on," was all the warning he gave before he put his foot down and peeled away from the curb.

/~/~/~/~/

Sebastian was sitting at the bar nursing a coffee when Malacai wandered back in. "He liked it then?" He asked as Malacai poured his own cup.

"Oh, he loved it. He's out in it now, with my mate a willing passenger. But I'm failing to see how buying your mate a car is going to win you any brownie points," Malacai said. "All you've done is given him a means to disappear whenever he wants."

"He could do that anyway." Sebastian grinned. "But he's got to come and say thank you, right? And he couldn't turn down the opportunity to help a mate either."

"I don't get it." Malacai frowned.

Sebastian leaned closer. "I can't drive. Never saw the point. But now Madison has a shiny new car, do you think he'd be inclined to help me learn?"

"You're a sneaky bastard. I like it." Malacai toasted him with his coffee mug. "Just don't break his heart, all right? Or you wouldn't be safe here ever again."

"Duly noted." Sebastian sat quietly, watching the goings on in the club, sipping his coffee and thinking about his next plan to woo the elusive Madison. Driving lessons were one thing, but planning to live with the pack was something else entirely. It seemed Malacai was a bit of a mind reader.

"What are you going to do with yourself, once you've claimed Madison? You know he won't leave here. He's worked damned hard to get to where he is today."

Sebastian hadn't said anything about claiming Madison, although it was looking more and more inevitable. There was a rod of steel in his mate's back that he had to respect and he'd enjoyed their date even if he did push too hard at the end of it. The thought certainly didn't scare him anymore.

"I don't need money," he said, voicing his thoughts. "But I'm not used to sitting around doing nothing. Madison works hard and keeps long hours. Is there anything around here you'd suggest I could do?"

"We can always use a man like you as a bouncer," Malacai said, "but I think while Madison is out, you should talk to Lucius and Vincent."

Sebastian tilted his head. "They run the club don't they; now Damien and Scott are living at the pack house."

"Exactly, and for a while, Lucius was happy to do it and Vincent didn't seem to mind. But running this place is a full-time job, as Madison will tell you. Vincent misses his family and wants more time to visit his home pack. He's even talking about adopting a couple of kids. They'd need to live with the pack for that."

"And what does Lucius think?"

"Lucius doesn't want to upset Damien or let him down, but he wants Vincent to be happy. I think if you offered him a way out, he might take it."

"But I'm not pack," Sebastian said, even as his mind ticked over the possibilities. Running a club wouldn't be so bad.

"Everyone knows Madison pretty much runs this place single-handedly. But because he was a sub here, too many of the Doms would give him a hard time if he was in charge. That's the only reason Damien didn't give him the job when he wanted out. He doesn't want to close the place. It's been his baby for well over a hundred years. If you had a chat with Lucius and Vincent...well, it's just a thought. Of course, that's assuming you are going to claim Madison. Claiming him would give you pack status and yes, Damien is going to want the club run by a pack member."

"Why didn't you take the job?" Malacai was the epitome of an older wolf shifter. Still looking as though he was in his thirties,

Sebastian knew the man was a lot older. He'd been by Damien's side for a long time and was well respected in the pack.

"Elijah. Being the only doctor we have, he needs to be on pack grounds most of the time and he's not that keen on the club scene." Malacai shrugged. "I didn't mind all this when I was single," he said, waving his hand at the crowds of people coming in for lunch. "But yep, I'm not ashamed to admit being curled up on the couch watching a movie with my mate is a lot more fun for me these days."

"You're getting old," Sebastian grinned as he put his mug on the bar and stood up. "I'll go and see if Lucius is in the office. Can you let Madison know I'll be in the apartment later if he's interested in finding me?"

Malacai laughed and nodded. "Madison's too polite not to come and say thank you."

"I'm counting on it." There was a decided spring in his step as Sebastian went to try and fit another piece in his future life puzzle.

Chapter Thirteen

Madison stepped into the club just over an hour later. Malacai, of course, was waiting and Elijah happily ran into his arms, his excited chatter swallowed by Malacai's rather demanding kisses. Madison felt a pang, nothing unusual there, but he was also happy. He realized he hadn't had fun in a really long time, and he wanted to share his good mood with someone.

"Is Sebastian around?" he asked when Malacai came up for air.

"He's probably back in his apartment. I think he's hoping you'd stop by."

"He bought me a car, it'd be rude not to." Madison worried that he was being manipulated, but the thrill of driving a fast car and the wind ruffling his hair was pounding through his veins; he hurried through the club and ran up the stairs to the apartments above.

One sharp knock at the door and Sebastian was there, as tall, sharp and droolworthy as ever. For a second, Madison hesitated but then he gave into his instincts. Jumping up he clung to Sebastian's shoulders and planted a soft, mouth-definitely-closed kiss on the stunned man's lips. Sebastian's arms came around him quickly, pulling their bodies flush together.

"I was just saying thank you for the car. It was a lovely surprise," Madison said, fighting to stop his voice from squeaking.

"So was the kiss," Sebastian said, his deep voice rumbling through Madison's body. "It's only fair I thank you for that, too."

Oh, he's good, Madison thought as a firm hand cupped the back of his head and Sebastian's lips were on his. *Too good,* he thought when

Sebastian managed to nudge his lips apart. Madison moaned as the taste from Sebastian's tongue flooded his mouth, causing his body to heat. *I'm in trouble.* Somehow his arms were wrapped around Sebastian's neck and with the pressure of the man's hand on his butt, he was trembling to stop the urge to rut against the solid body.

/~/~/~/~/

Sebastian knew he should stop. He didn't even enjoy kissing, for fuck's sake. But from the moment he saw Madison at the door, his cheeks flushed, his hair in a tangle and a smile on his beautiful face Sebastian felt something in his heart shift. And something else changed too. He suddenly found he didn't want to set Madison down. In fact, he was a little worried he might never want to let him out of his arms again.

Then there was the matter of them still being in an open doorway. An amused cough from a passing pack member reminded him of that. Groaning, his lips still exploring Madison's mouth, he spun around and kicked the apartment door closed. Madison leaned back.

"Oh my god, oh my god, this should stop," he panted.

"Did you want to stop?" Sebastian wasn't sure where his mind was at, but his cock was more than happy to play.

"Yes. No. Shit. Let me down. I can't think when all I can smell is you." Madison shimmied out of his arms and adjusted the lump in his pants. Sebastian felt a sudden chill as though he was missing something.

"It's the mating bond," Madison said, his face bright red, his chest heaving. "You can't help it. I can't help it. It's just what it is. I'd better go. I'm sorry."

"You don't have to." Sebastian stepped closer. "We both want this. Why not let nature take its course? We're both adults."

Madison growled and for the first time, Sebastian saw the light of his wolf flashing in his eyes. It changed Madison's aura, made him seem stronger and more menacing and Sebastian reminded himself Madison wasn't human. A strong predator lurked under his mate's coiffured exterior.

That was even more apparent when Madison spoke. "You don't get it, do you? You dumb fuck. Claiming is everything to a wolf shifter. Shifters wait their whole lives desperate to meet the other half of their soul. I'm over sixty years old," Sebastian's jaw dropped. "Sixty years I've been waiting for that one person who'd treat me right, love me in the way

I knew I deserved. I kept waiting. Kept hoping and then I scented you and I knew my search was over. Except you just want to get your rocks off. You have no intention of claiming me because your heart belongs to fucking Alexander. I know that because you told me!"

"I...."

"NO!" Madison stamped his foot. "Just no, all right. I want you, of course I do. But I don't want to just go to bed with you. I know the sex will be amazing, it always is between mates. But I want more than that. I want to know what your favorite color is, what music you like to listen to. I want movie nights, dates and the whole fucking shooting match. My wolf yearns for you; he aches to see our mark on your neck. It's taking all my energy not to shift and bite you and to hell with the consequences. But you've already made it plain you don't want that and I...I can't...I'm not going to let you keep playing around with me anymore."

He spun around and was out the door before Sebastian could blink. "My favorite color is blue," Sebastian whispered, his hand outstretched towards the door. He'd always loved blue because it was the color of Alexander's eyes but now as he stared at the empty doorway, he knew that shift in his heart was Alexander moving over. It was Madison's eyes he wanted to see sparkle with passion. It was his laughter he wanted to hear.

"You should go and talk to him."

Spinning around, Sebastian growled to see Lasse lounging on his bed eating a handful of grapes. "What have I told you about eavesdropping on personal conversations? Haven't you got better things to do?"

"Nope and it's a good thing I'm here, you could use some advice," Lasse said, not at all put out by Sebastian's anger. "You need to go after that young man. You need to take him somewhere quiet, sit him down and talk to him. Really talk to him, or you're going to lose him."

"I was going to claim him," Sebastian half-turned towards the door as if hoping Madison would come back. "I wouldn't have taken him to bed and not claimed him at the same time. I bought him a car so he could teach me to drive. I've spoken to Lucius about taking over the running of this club so I can be with him every day. I did all this for him."

"I'm glad you've finally come to your senses," Lasse said, popping another grape into his mouth. "There's just one thing you forgot to do."

"What's that?"

"You didn't tell him what those plans were."

"Shit." Sebastian ran out of the room, hoping to see where Madison had gone. But his mate wasn't in the building. Rubbing a hidden tattoo on the back of his hand, he materialized in his dad's house, but Madison didn't appear to be in the underworld either. Where the heck would he have gone? Then Sebastian angled his head, listening carefully – the eerie sound of a lone wolf howl pierced the silence.

"Fucking hell, he's gone outside. Dad should've warned him." Clicking his fingers, Sebastian summoned his broadsword and sprinted out of his father's mansion. It wasn't only demons, snakes and the hellhounds that were dangerous in his father's domain. Bitter spirits lingered to cause strife to the innocent; the Arae, angry curse demons could make life a living hell and that's without the familiars of Eurynomas wandering around. Their rotting corpses would be hell on a wolf's sensitive nose.

Thanatos kept his grass green. Sebastian had no idea how much magic that entailed, but his dad always said he liked a bit of color. Standing on the edge of it, a barren red landscape rolled for miles in front of him, broken occasionally by the twisted remains of a building and clumps of blackened trees. Sebastian inclined his head, listening for a howl. There. Over in the trees. Snake country. Not good.

As Thanatos's son, Sebastian grew up in the rugged landscape. This was his world which meant his magic was stronger and he could translocate himself. A quick click and he was surrounded by trees, their black twisted limbs a mockery of their living cousins on earth.

"Madison," he called out softly. "Madison, you really shouldn't be out here."

There was a snarl to his left. Hacking his way through gnarled brambles, Sebastian stopped at the sight of a pure white wolf standing over the remains of a large python. The wolf's lips curled back and he snarled as Sebastian got closer.

"Madison, are you in there, mate? This is not a good place for you to be. Didn't Dad warn you never to step off the lawn?"

The wolf snarled again, his ears flicking back and forth. It was Madison all right. For one thing, every creature in the Underworld was black or dull shades of gray. Madison's fur stood out like a neon sign in a ghost town. But it was the eyes that let Sebastian know he'd found his mate. Brilliant blue, they were fixed on him and he shivered; knowing what prey felt like now.

"We need to talk, Madison," he said calmly. "I think you got the wrong idea earlier. I've been making plans for our life together, but I guess I should have discussed them with you first."

The wolf cocked his head slightly, but his teeth were still showing. "How about we go back to Dad's...." That was as far as he got because with a vicious snarl, Madison leaped. Sebastian braced himself, sure he was about to feel those razor-sharp teeth, but Madison flew past him and locked his jaws around a fucking hellhound of all things, who'd been sneaking up on him.

"Stop, Hellhound," Sebastian yelled. "In the name of my father Thanatos, I command you to stop." But the hound didn't listen. There weren't any others nearby, meaning this one had probably been driven from the pack. Rogues weren't common, but without an alpha, they often went insane. Sebastian watched helplessly, his sword useless in his hand, as the two similar sized animals, rolled around each other, biting and clawing at each other furiously.

Madison's fur was streaked with dust and blood, but he was holding his own. His growls were fierce and he moved fast, snapping and tearing at every inch of skin he could reach. The rogue hound was crazed; spittle flying from his massive jaws, but there was no method in his attack. His bright red eyes flashed as he kept trying to lunge at Madison; but Madison jumped on his back, pushing the hound to the ground, the crunch of bone loud as Madison's teeth severed his spine.

Sebastian bent over, resting his hands on his knees. He didn't realize he'd stopped breathing and now he felt dizzy as if his legs wouldn't hold him. "Madison, please tell me you're all right. Oh fuck, you saved me from being badly injured. Please tell me he didn't bite you."

Soft fur brushed around his legs, almost knocking him over. "Can I, is it okay to touch you?" A warm nose on his neck seemed permission enough. Sebastian sank to his knees and wrapped his arms around Madison's furry neck. "You protected me," he whispered. "Just like any warrior mate would. You also scared the shit out of me."

The wolf woofed in his ear, making Sebastian jump. "You know I'm yours, don't you? You really are cognizant in this form." The wolf nodded and pushed closer, rubbing his face and neck over every inch of exposed skin. Sebastian laughed. "You're also filthy although for some reason it's easier to talk to you this way," he said, pulling the collar of his shirt aside. "Mark me, you gorgeous wolf. I know you want to. Mark me as yours and then we'll worry about what your human side has to say about it later."

Madison looked at him, his head slanted to one side, his ears forward. "I mean it," Sebastian said. "I didn't mean to hurt you or your human side. I've been thoughtless and hurtful and you'll have to put up with that until I learn to do better. But please, I know how important this mark is to you and I want you to do it."

The wolf carefully rested his jaws over the dip between neck and shoulder. Sebastian braced himself for the pain, knowing the wolf could rip his throat out in an instant if he wanted. There was a sharp sting as Madison bit and to Sebastian's surprise his cock was suddenly hard and without warning he climaxed, creating one hell of a mess in his pants. Sebastian panted as he rested his head on

Madison's neck, his head dizzy from the sudden blood drain to his cock. The wolf cleaned the wound with long loving licks as Sebastian tried to catch his breath. He wasn't sure how he felt about wolf drool, but the wolf seemed happy.

"There's a buzzing in my head," he said when he could finally speak.

It will settle down once you've claimed me, Madison's disapproving voice rang loud and clear in his head. *A shifter claims through sex and a bite. But don't worry,* he added as Sebastian stiffened, *my wolf's not interested in having sex with you. That's what our human side enjoys. I wouldn't have let him bite you at all, but he's so damn pleased with himself. He thinks he saved your life.*

"He saved me from a world of hurt," Sebastian agreed, looking at the rogue's body. "Fancy a shower and dinner?"

Are you going to talk to me? Madison's voice sounded sad. *I don't know what's going on with you. What changed your mind? When? Why? You know this is binding, right? You can't get out of it. I'm so confused.*

Sebastian cupped the wolf's lovely head carefully in his hands. "I was a fool," he said clearly and simply. "I made a snap judgment about you and I've quickly learned how wrong I was. I am sorry. I will be very proud to call you mate if you'll have me."

It's a bit late to worry about that side of things now. Madison's sardonic reply made Sebastian smile. *That bite will scar and will never fade.*

"But are you happy about it?" Madison's prancing step and happily wagging tail as they made their way back to Thanatos's house was answer enough. The wolf side of his shifter was happy, now all

Sebastian had to do was convince the very human Madison that mating with him was a good idea.

Chapter Fourteen

Madison groaned as the hot water hit his aching muscles. He didn't think he'd ever been so tired in his life. But then it had to have been twenty years since he'd fought in wolf form. "Oh, I am going to suffer for this in the morning," he muttered. "Snakes, fucking big dogs, what the hell was I thinking? That snake was just nasty." He shuddered under the water as he recalled the taste.

Truthfully, Madison was glad he had a moment to himself. Sebastian said he was going to fix dinner and aside from a gentle kiss, delivered after Madison shifted, he hadn't said or done anything else. Madison wondered if he was regretting the offer to be bitten. After the warrior statement Sebastian made, the claiming smacked of a gift given after battle, rather than a carefully thought out proposal.

"He said he'd planned to claim me anyway," Madison's hopeful side said.

"He hasn't said anything about Alexander," his cynical side replied.

"Isn't that something he needs to work out for himself?" Madison's hopeful side was an eternal optimist and didn't get a voice very often.

"Probably just wants a fuck and will disappear before the cum dries," his cynical side had seen that happen more than once.

"Or maybe we just wait and see. Now shut up." Madison muttered, grabbing his washcloth and slathering it with the fragrant soap gel he loved. He was hungry. His wolf was tired and curled up happy in his mind. The shower was decadent, he had a lovely robe to put on afterward and yeah, *I'm going to take today as a win,* he decided firmly.

/~/~/~/~/

Sebastian swayed his hips slowly in time to the music as he grilled steaks and found salad in the fridge. The buzz he had in his head was still there, but he hadn't heard Madison talking to him through their link since wolf became man.

What have I done? I claimed a mate. It's permanent, and with both of them immortal, there'd be no going back or one dying so the other one could be free. *Am I an idiot or what?*

The strange thing was, Sebastian didn't feel panicked. It was almost as though his reluctance to mate was a habit he'd cultivated since his dad pulled him from Alexander's side. After so much time, it was surprisingly easy for him to push those doubts aside as well. If anything, he realized as he flipped the steaks, remembering Madison would want his almost raw, he was relaxed, settled and calmer than he'd been for a long time.

I'm mated. Sebastian tested the idea in his head again. No panic. No sudden surges of anger. Yes, there was the little matter of Sebastian making his claim too, but for all intents and purposes, the hard part was done. He'd made the commitment. Sebastian realized his life was going to change and he sincerely hoped it would be for the better.

For centuries, he'd felt like the poor relation. He was the son of a godly being, but unlike Lasse, Nereus or even Baby, only half of his genetics came from the gods. Sebastian had no idea who his mother was. Thanatos said nothing about her except she was human and died during childbirth. Given that his father was Death, Sebastian recognized it was a sad topic for his dad and never asked anything more about her.

The consequences of that pairing meant while his powers worked in the Underworld, they didn't translate on earth. He could call things to him while he was on earth, but he couldn't create things. He couldn't translocate himself like Poseidon's sons could. They never made him feel bad about it, but it used to frustrate Sebastian sometimes. It was like he wasn't human, but he wasn't a true demigod either.

And now his life had changed completely. It'd been coming a long, long time. Nereus used to spend hours, usually while he was drunk, dreaming of his mate. He just could never decide what type of mate he wanted. Sebastian grinned as he flipped the steaks onto a platter to rest. Nereus got the pretty twink he wanted, but Sebastian was still curious what his second mate would be like. Maybe once Madison taught him to drive, they could visit Cloverleah and he could see for himself.

I'm used to living as a human, he reminded himself as he hunted in the fridge for beer. *Living in a pack won't be much different than living in military camps or when we were on campaign.* The sadness Sebastian usually felt when he remembered those days, centuries ago, was missing. If anything, he felt a spark of hope for the future.

There was a rustle of silk on skin and Sebastian looked up to see Madison standing at the doorway. "I could smell meat cooking," Madison said shyly. "Is it okay to come in?"

"Grab the salad bowl and the cutlery and we'll eat in the living room," he said, picking up the meat platter. "No point in being stuffy at the table when it's just the two of us unless you're expecting Dad as well at some point this evening."

"He's tracking his mate," Madison said with a grin. "Seems the Fates have been busy lately."

They have indeed, but Sebastian's mind emptied of any thoughts of his father, as Madison moved in front of him, his sexy ass rubbing against the green silk of the robe he was wearing. *I do hope you're naked under there,* he thought. With any luck, dinner would be over quickly and if he played his cards right, Madison might be keen on an early night. *Talk first,* he reminded himself crossly. *Talk first, but talk fast.* He owed his mate that much and now the claiming was nothing but a formality; Sebastian wanted to show his mate just how much he'd been thinking about their life together.

/~/~/~/~/

Madison was determined to be calm. No matter what Sebastian said, he'd listen. He knew he tended to overreact occasionally, but the sight of Sebastian on his knees, fear, and relief etched on his handsome face after his tussle with the dog from hell had a powerful impact on Madison. He would be an adult. He would listen and he'd pray in silence to every deity in existence Sebastian didn't break him now.

This was why he was nervous; Sebastian had that power especially now he'd been claimed by Madison's wolf. He tried to focus on the food, which was difficult with his mate's scent teasing his nose. The steak was delicious, lightly seasoned and grilled to perfection. Madison wasn't keen on salads, but Sebastian found fresh rolls and butter so he wasn't just eating meat. It seemed they'd both decided not to talk about anything heavy until after the meal, and Madison appreciated the courtesy.

When the plates were cleared, Madison resorted to fiddling with the edge of his robe until Sebastian handed him a mug of coffee.

"Okay, this is it." Sebastian put down his mug and rubbed his hands on his jeans.

Is he nervous too?

"I'm apologizing now for anything I say that might hurt you," Sebastian said slowly. "I don't have a filter. I tend to be very blunt, but please hear me out. My intention is to share information with you, not hurt you so please don't take anything I say as a personal attack."

Not an auspicious beginning, Madison thought, but he nodded to show he understood. The coffee was delicious and strong enough to provide him with the shot of caffeine he desperately needed.

"As you know, I fell in love with Alexander the Great. History

records my name as Hephaestion."
Sebastian looked at Madison to see
if the name meant anything and
Madison nodded. He wasn't stupid;
he'd Googled Alexander the Great
as soon as Sebastian mentioned
him.

"You are known in the records as
good friends," Madison said.

"Those histories were written well
after our time," Sebastian laughed.
"By the time the histories were
recorded, a man laying with
another man was considered sinful
and of course, Alexander's memory
couldn't be tainted with anything
like that. We were together a long
time." Sebastian fell silent and
Madison watched him closely.
Whatever his faults, it was clear his
mate loved the damned man and
there was nothing Madison could
do about it now.

"Anyhow," Sebastian pulled himself
together, "I was in love, I thought
Alexander was too. We weren't

mates, and I knew I was destined for one, but I was also a lot younger and figured I wasn't going to be ruled by the Fates or my father's wishes. Our friendship persisted despite Alexander's marriages; women didn't come on campaigns. I was by his side in all things that mattered and as his fame and fortune grew, I used to dream of making him immortal so he and I could rule forever."

Personally, Madison thought that was a bit idealistic. People would notice their lack of aging and they'd just as likely to be burned at the stake for witchcraft or consorting with the devil. However, his knowledge of history was sketchy at best and he motioned Sebastian to continue.

"The Fates had other ideas," Sebastian said and there was a slight catch in his voice. "They sent Alexander a mate in the form of Bagoas. Stunningly beautiful, blond and so tiny he couldn't hold a broadsword if his life depended on it. A cat shifter of all things and of course he knew immediately that Alexander was his. Alexander didn't put up much of a fight," he added bitterly.

"What did you do?" Madison had a strong urge to give Bagoas a huge hooray, but he stayed silent.

"I went to my father and pleaded with him," Sebastian said. "Dad speaks to the Fates. I was sure if he said something, the Fates would change their minds about us. Alexander made the world a better place. Imagine what he could do if he was immortal."

Madison didn't want to imagine it. In fact, he shuddered at the thought. "I take it, Dad didn't agree?"

"No, he didn't," Sebastian's voice turned brittle as he stood and started pacing. "He said Alexander would change the course of history if he didn't follow his life thread to the end. Told me I had to respect his mating with Bagoas and leave things alone. I wanted to kill the little shit."

"And did you?" History never mentioned what happened to Bagoas and Madison had wondered. He leaned back against the couch, his clenched fists hidden in the folds of his robe.

"Nope, Dad fucked that up for me too. He killed me off. Me, his only son! Poisoned my food so badly my body shut down and I ended up back here. By the time I was well enough to go back, Alexander had buried my body and turned to Bagoas in his grief. The only joy I got out of any of it was Alexander didn't live long after my supposed death. While I mourned him desperately at least Bagoas didn't have him either. I laughed when Bagoas died. Being a shifter, he was gone within a month of Alexander. It was the will of the Fates, my dad said and that was fucking that."

Madison was silent for a moment, getting his immediate response, which was to tear Sebastian a new asshole for being an asshole, under control. When he was confident he could open his mouth without being rude, he said quietly, "Did this experience sour you against fated mates, twinks or both?"

"I understand the concept of mating." Sebastian was still yelling. "But tell me, just tell me, how the hell some tiny little twink like Bagoas be the perfect mate for a warrior like Alexander. How do the Fates work this shit out? Alexander was a fighter, a real man and they sent him a tiny cat shifter who sang and danced and played with flowers."

Madison couldn't look at Sebastian, he was so angry at his mate's callous disregard for poor Bagoas. He focused on his fingers instead. "Shawn, the shifter guardian from Cloverleah, told me once that mates weren't meant to be clones of each other," he said as calmly as he could. "They are two halves that fit together to become whole again. Even a warrior needs to laugh sometimes or be entertained and as a shifter, Bagoas would have been strong in a way that might not have been clear to the people around him." He should know. People often underestimated him and then wished they hadn't.

"You really believe that? Are you implying me and Alexander were too much alike and that's why we couldn't be mates? We were perfect for each other." The scorn on Sebastian's face hit Madison like a knife to the gut and broke his control.

"I think the human died over two thousand years ago and you should let it go," he snapped. "The reason a shifter dies so soon after his mate isn't just because the animal side pines for them. That's a Fate fail-safe so the pair can reincarnate or spend the afterlife together. It means that in the centuries you've been pining over someone else's mate, Alexander and Bagoas have spent at least twenty lifetimes together as mates and once Alexander died that first time, his memory of you would have died too. Don't you get it?" Madison was on his feet now, uncaring that his robe fell open. His body was nothing to be ashamed of. "All this time you've been harboring this hatred for twinks and people shorter than you. I bet you've never fucked anyone under six feet tall and what a waste, an absolute waste. You have no idea what you're missing. Your heart is so full of hate and anger that you've never once considered that the other parties in this major drama of yours have already moved on and have lived countless happy lives together. The only one who isn't happy is you." *And me,* he thought, but Madison wasn't going to say that.

"You...wait...reincarnation?" The anger drained from Sebastian's body so fast he fell into the nearest chair, his face pale. "All this time Alexander's been living lives without me?"

"You aren't his mate. You were never meant to be together more than in that one lifetime." Madison perched on the edge of the couch, pulling his robe over his legs. "It's only mates that come back together and share multiple lives; at least, that's what Shawn said."

"Why didn't Dad tell me? I thought...humans don't...at least I didn't think they did," Sebastian whispered.

"Would you have listened? Look, I don't know about humans, they have lots of different beliefs. I'm a shifter and I believe what a shifter guardian tells me. A mate is a mate is a mate. Our forms might change with different lives, the way we meet our mate is different every time, but there is always that part of our soul that knows we've known a person before, even if we can't remember how or why. Or at least it's supposed to be like that," Madison frowned. "I didn't feel that part of it when I met you, but then you're immortal so you couldn't have been my mate if I'd lived before. Guess it's not really important if I'm never going to die now."

"I'm sorry," Sebastian said suddenly.

Madison shook his head. "What about specifically?" He asked cautiously.

"That I'm the one you got stuck with." Sebastian's head was down and Madison cursed his wolf who wanted to comfort their mate. He got up and slid onto Sebastian's lap, wrapping his arms around broad shoulders.

"What are you doing? I thought you were angry with me." Sebastian looked up in surprise.

"I have every reason to be angry with you, but I don't carry it around for a gazillion years like you do. I am giving *my* warrior a hug because he looks like he needs it. You know, big guys never mention it, but I have it on good authority I'm a damned good hugger and everyone needs one sometimes whether they admit it or not."

"I can certainly see the benefits." Sebastian rested his head on Madison's shoulder and Madison ran his fingers up his mate's strong neck. With the close proximity, his body reacted instinctively, but Madison pushed his naughty thoughts away and focused on comforting a warrior who'd carried ridiculous self-imposed burdens for far too long.

Chapter Fifteen

Sebastian was furious at himself. He'd promised he wouldn't say stuff to upset his new mate, and then one mention of that cat shifting slinky b...yeah, he needed to stop doing that. His new mate was holding him, comforting him despite his harsh words, and Sebastian was an intelligent man. Nereus's words about his smaller mate cherishing him and showing he cared ran through his head and in that moment, he totally got it.

It felt strange having a much smaller man settled on his lap. Not that his hookups were much for lap sitting. His warriors grunted, slapped each other around as if almost ashamed of showing any softness. This...the fingers on his neck, the comfort of Madison's slight frame...it was nice, soothing and yet combined with the silkiness of his robe, and the heat from

Madison's skin, it was also as hot as hell.

"I...er...you're not wearing anything under that robe," Sebastian said awkwardly sitting up and watching his mate's face.

Madison shrugged. "Didn't see the point," he said with a small smile. "Shifters don't wear underwear as a rule and I assumed you had the same idea I did about how this evening would end. Or is having sex with a smaller, younger guy going to ruin your reputation?"

Sebastian knew Madison was teasing, but he growled all the same. His cock was hard enough to pound rocks and his earlier anger had morphed into a sexual energy which was now focused on how soon he could find a flat surface. *Bed,* he reminded himself, *this isn't a hookup,* but then his brain shutdown as Madison's soft lips tickled his jaw line.

"Such a hard man," Madison whispered against his skin. "Hard, stern and always in control," his feather light touches sent tingles down Sebastian's spine. Strong fingers moved from the back of his neck around to the front, slowly heading down, tracing his torso as Sebastian's shirt was opened one button at a time.

"Hard all over," Madison's mouth followed the trail set by his fingers and Sebastian leaned back in the chair instinctively. His urge to lunge, grab and fuck grew, but Madison's touch was addictive. He wanted more but he didn't want it to stop.

"Hmm," Madison chuckled against his abs and Sebastian stifled a groan as he felt a flick of tongue. "Your muscles are so tense. I don't know if you want to throw me off, or throw me down and fuck me till I beg for mercy."

Those simple words painted such a vivid visual Sebastian's hips left the chair. He bit his lip and gripped the armrests so tight the material under his fingers gave way. Madison took that moment to suckle the end of his cock, *when did he undo my pants?* Although Sebastian didn't have the brain power to answer his own questions, he was too busy...nope, too late. His mouth opened.

Moans and curses fell from his lips as Madison explored his cock. Sebastian registered the weight falling from his knees as Madison slipped to the floor, his hands and mouth busy teasing and driving Sebastian to the brink of madness.

"You...you...." Nope, he couldn't form a sentence, but Madison looked up, a demure smile on his face.

"Did you want me to stop?"

"Yes, no, damn it, aaargh."

Madison swallowed him whole; the sensation of his cockhead grazing his mate's throat sent Sebastian's body into a frenzy. He wanted to thrust; it was in his nature for fuck's sake, but Madison had a surprisingly strong grip on his hips and was holding him firm. And it seemed like he was directly connected to Sebastian's psyche, his inner desires; the hint of teeth under his glans, the slather of tongue adding extra sensations on every downward slide. When Sebastian felt the slight sting of claws run across his tight balls, he erupted with a roar; Madison's head bobbing slightly as he swallowed every drop.

Sebastian flopped back into the chair, his chest heaving. He was still half-dressed, his shirt pushed open but still caught on his arms; his jeans undone and nothing but his balls and half-hard cock exposed. Madison sat like an angel between his legs, still licking his swollen lips.

"Feel better?" Madison asked.

"Good enough to know we need a bed darned fast. You've had your fun and now it's my turn. I have some claiming to do."

/~/~/~/~/

Madison had every reason to feel pleased with himself. He'd turned his tightly buttoned mate into a moaning mess and as he didn't think that was remotely possible, he took Sebastian's orgasm as a personal achievement. But as he led his huge mate into the bedroom Thanatos gave him he felt nervous. Sebastian reminded him of Damien in so many ways and he guessed their sexual techniques were probably similar.

It was in that frame of mind; Madison carefully took off his robe and laid it gently on a chair before hunting out a new tube of lube he knew was in the bedside drawer. He turned to see Sebastian butt naked staring at him with a feral expression that made Madison gulp.

He held up the lube. "Did you want to do this, or should I?" He remembered Damien never had patience for prep.

Sebastian smirked. "Throw that on the bed."

What? Madison was so far to the right of the virgin scale it wasn't funny, but it'd been a while. Gritting his teeth, because he was a wolf shifter, after all, he threw the lube within reaching distance and arranged himself over the edge of the bed. *Better than Damien's desk,* he thought as he arranged his elbows on the plush comforter and rested his head on them. Thanks to Sebastian's scent that still teased his nose his cock was hard enough and as they were mates and he wasn't a sub anymore, there was a good chance he'd be allowed to come at least. But he still couldn't resist a small sigh as he heard Sebastian come up behind him.

"You look very beautiful like this," Sebastian crooned and Madison felt a rough hand run up his thigh. "I bet there's been many a man brought to his knees by the sight of your ass displayed in such a tempting fashion."

Madison bit his arm to stop from growling. It wasn't as though Sebastian claimed virginity status either.

"Hmm, so beautiful and all totally mine." There were two hands on Madison's butt cheeks forcing them apart. Madison forced his breathing to stay slow and calm as a thumb brushed across his opening. "All those men, even Damien I hear," Sebastian continued in a conversational tone. "You just bend over and take whatever's thrust in your direction."

Madison turned his head, harsh words ringing through his head. He was a damn good bottom and he wouldn't be insulted for it. But Sebastian didn't give him a chance to speak. "Don't you think with a mate, you'd offer more?" He asked as Madison found himself spun around and thrown into the middle of the bed, landing on his back.

"Don't you think, as your mate, I believe you deserve more than that?" Sebastian loomed over him, his gray eyes dark with passion. "That maybe I don't just want a hole to plug, but a partner in my arms; a man who'll look at me with those bright blue eyes and show me without words how much he wants me?"

Madison was confused and he was sure it showed on his face. He tentatively raised his arms, draping them over Sebastian's shoulders.

"I want you to see me," Sebastian's voice dropped into a growl. "I want all your responses. I want to know you're aware every second we're together that I'm the one wringing the pleasure from your body. That I am the only one that will from this moment on."

Madison didn't have the words to respond but when Sebastian's harsh lips met his he used his body to say the things in his heart. Sebastian's hands were firm, leaving trails of heat across his skin. His mouth was ravaged over and over again. Hard abs teased his cock, never quite giving him the relief Madison was desperate for, and it seemed like an eternity before he felt a slick finger breach his hole.

"Oh thank god, please," Madison moaned against Sebastian's neck. Sebastian's chest blanketed his as if pinning him to the bed. *Like I'm going anywhere.* He spread his legs as wide as possible, silently pleading for Sebastian to move.

A grunted "pillow" had Madison scrabbling with his hand above him. In his haste, he grabbed two and succeeded in knocking his mate around the head with them, but Sebastian was at least focused on what he was doing. Madison felt his ass lifted and then Sebastian settled between his legs. *Finally.*

"Do you want me?"

Madison rolled his eyes and growled. He'd deal with Sebastian's insecurity issues later. "Get in there," he said, hoping he managed a modicum of civility in his tone. From Sebastian's raised eyebrows he guessed he failed in that attempt, but a nudge against his ass grabbed his attention and held it. Madison barely breathed as Sebastian breached him for the first time.

"Holy fuck," Sebastian breathed out as his entire length filled Madison in seconds. Madison would have seconded the sentiment but he was too full to talk. In that instant, all the emptiness in his life disappeared and he clung to Sebastian's biceps just trying to breathe.

"I never dreamed," Sebastian's voice was full of wonder. "You...I feel it. Really feel it. I've never..."

Madison didn't want to interrupt Sebastian's wonder at whatever, but he had needs of his own. "Move, damn it, we can talk about it later."

He thought Sebastian would be angry but his mate smiled, really smiled and Madison memorized every fleck in those gray eyes as Sebastian gently rocked in and out of his body. It was...sensual, Madison decided. Not what he was used to, but as Sebastian slightly quickened the pace, Madison could see how slow and steady would win the race. Propped up as he was, Madison couldn't thrust back, but he did manage to squeeze his inner muscles every now and then to spur his lover along.

Sebastian seemed equally enthralled. Not once did Madison have to wonder if his mate's mind flickered back to a long dead lover. Sebastian's eyes were firmly focused on him and as he sped up and the biceps under Madison's hands started to tremble slightly, Madison felt a fire burn in his gut and his heart filled.

"Don't stop," he whispered.

"Never," Sebastian promised and for some reason, the words seem to inflame his lover and Madison cried out as Sebastian pounded into him in earnest. A spark was lit from his belly to his lower spine and Madison threw his head back and yelled, "Sebastian!" as his cock exploded between them.

Sebastian's thrusts stuttered and then he tipped his head back and invoked in a loud voice, "As the true son of Thanatos, with the blessings of the Fates, I claim the shifter known as Madison as my one, my only, my true mate."

A gust of wind blew around the room and somewhere in the distance came the baying of hounds. The dull red glare outside the window flared brightly and Sebastian laughed as Madison felt his insides creamed.

"Yes, it's done," Sebastian panted. "Look."

Madison followed Sebastian's eyes which were fixated on his chest. The scythe of the grim reaper was emblazoned in red across his heart. "It's a pretty color," he said tracing the lines gently.

Still chuckling, Sebastian rested on one side, his fingers following Madison's. "You are now a true being of the Underworld. The pack hounds will obey your call and all who reside here will know if they mess with you, they will incur the wrath of me and Dad. You've now become a Prince of Death, just like me."

Madison wrinkled his nose as he thought about it. "Does that mean I need new outfits? Only, I like a bit of color in my clothes. And I don't have to have black hair, do I? Because there is a decided dearth of blond in this place I've noticed but I'm not coloring my hair just to fit in."

"Oh Madison, you are truly perfect," Sebastian laughed. "Don't change a thing. You're perfect just the way you are."

Madison knew he would worry about his new position later, but for now, he comforted himself with curling up in his mate's arms and letting Sebastian hold him as he drifted off to sleep. *Those hounds are damn loud*, he thought. *I wonder if there's any way to shut them up.* The noise stopped. Spooky.

Chapter Sixteen

Sebastian lazily opened his eyes to the sight of Madison rushing around like a mad thing. "Where's the fire?" He grumbled as he rolled and stretched, working out a few kinks in his back.

"I was due at work twenty minutes ago," Madison said frantically messing with his hair in the mirror. Sebastian fought the urge to drag his mate back to bed. Somehow, he didn't think his immaculate mate would appreciate it.

"I'm sure Lucius won't mind. He's leaving at the end of the week anyway," he said lazily, covering a yawn. "I said I would go in sometime today to start learning what needs to be done."

"He's expecting you today?" Madison screeched as he turned from the mirror. "What are you still doing in bed? The suppliers are due today, someone is stealing from the bar stock, Boris will be waiting to give me shit about something in his order because he's so damn picky about the meat he brings in and that's without the dozen or so 'relationship' issues that will have occurred overnight. I didn't get anything done yesterday thanks to you and your damn car, and you're lazing around like a big cat?"

Sebastian sat up. "How much of this stuff does Lucius deal with?"

"Lucius? Pff," Madison waved his hand. "The boss doesn't do any of that, but he has to be seen to be involved. He handles the investment meetings, schmoozing with the human council members in town and that sort of thing. I do the grunt work, but this is a pack situation. The club members are all pack, and they expect an Alpha-type to make the decisions."

"But you'll be with me, right?" Sebastian scratched his head. Lucius didn't mention any of this.

In fact, all Lucius said was to rely on Madison and everything would run smoothly.

"Well, not right this minute, obviously, because I'm dressed for work and you haven't even showered." Madison shook his head. "I'll go and make a start on getting things caught up from yesterday; you move your ass."

Sebastian groaned and slumped back on the bed as Madison strode off; a powerhouse vision in his Armani suit. It was his first day as a mated man and his mate had just gone to work. Had he done something wrong? Sebastian's visions of breakfast in bed and a lazy, sex-filled day were shattered. *Has Madison even had breakfast?*

Sighing, he rolled out of bed and headed for the bathroom. Running a club, he could do. Dealing with Dom/sub issues, no problem. Getting his workaholic mate to appreciate the virtues of spending a day in bed or even staying long enough to have breakfast might be damn near impossible.

/~/~/~/~/

Madison had been feeling guilty all morning about the way he left Sebastian. It wasn't what he wanted to do. He was newly mated and entitled to a minimum of three days off. But when he woke up he had a sudden attack of nerves. What if Sebastian regretted his decision? He hated the thought of them arguing on their first day. It just seemed so wrong. So, he did what he always did when he was unsure about something; he threw himself into his work.

"I didn't expect to see you in today. Did something go wrong with your mating?" Malacai knocked once and walked in.

Madison sighed. That had to be the tenth time someone had made a dig about his mated status. "I am mated," he said tersely pulling up a file on his tablet. "But I didn't get anything done yesterday. No one else seems capable of doing stuff. There was a mountain of paperwork on my desk this morning. It's not going to shift itself."

Malacai swung himself into the nearest chair, his gaze steady. Madison could try ignoring him, but he knew from experience it wouldn't do any good. "Yes?" He said, looking pointedly at his tablet.

"There's something different about you," Malacai observed.

Madison frowned. "A couple of people mentioned there's a change in my scent, which I would expect if I'd mated with a wolf, but I didn't. I'm not sure what you mean."

"Your scent is slightly different," Malacai agreed. "Sebastian didn't bite you, did he?"

"No, of course not. He left his father's mark on my chest. I assume it was through magic."

"Hmm," Malacai tilted his head, looking at him sideways. "My wolf wants to submit to you and yet neither of us can work out why and we both know that's not me being disrespectful, it's just the way of the pack. Has anyone else mentioned it?"

Shaking his head, Madison ran his hands over his jacket. "Not specifically. John in the bar seemed a bit nervy around me earlier, but I thought that was because of the thefts I was checking on."

Madison thought back over his morning. He interacted with a lot of pack members on a daily basis. "Boris didn't seem as angry as he usually is with me and...yeah, a couple of the Doms were waiting to complain when I got in this morning, but they suddenly decided they had somewhere else to go. They are always nitpicking about something, though. Do you think it's because I smell funny?"

"You don't smell funny," Malacai said quickly and Madison heaved a sigh of relief. "It's not even your scent exactly. You just seem...stronger somehow."

"I killed a snake and a hellhound in the Underworld yesterday. The hound was a rogue, but he was sneaking up on Sebastian and my wolf didn't like it. Maybe my wolf's still a bit edgy about it."

Malacai's eyes widened. "A hellhound?" He gasped. "You took on a hellhound by yourself and you killed him?"

"He was going to hurt Sebastian. I know the man's immortal but that beast could've done some damage." Madison didn't know what the problem was. Malacai would kill anyone that looked at Elijah the wrong way.

"And this was before you mated with Sebastian or after?"

"Before," Madison was getting uncomfortable. Malacai was looking at him like he'd developed a second head. "I don't know what the problem is. Thanatos told me I was immortal anyway. I wasn't going to die."

"We need to see Damien," Malacai said, standing and pulling out his phone.

"I've got work to do," Madison said helplessly staring at the mess on his desk. "I thought...Sebastian...."

"Sebastian is in with Lucius right now, ripping him a new one for apparently taking advantage of you and the things you do around here," Malacai said shortly, firing off a text. "It was what I came to tell you, but I think we have bigger problems than how much work you do."

"What do you mean?" Now Madison was worried. "I'm not going to get kicked out of the pack, am I? Damien knew me and Sebastian were mates, he never said I couldn't claim him."

"He wouldn't do that," Malacai nodded towards the door. "Come on. We'll go and see if Sebastian and Lucius have stopped fighting and then head out and meet Damien."

Fuck this day is going from bad to worse, Madison fretted as he followed the pack second down to Lucius's office. *I should have stayed in bed with my mate. Anything would be better than facing expulsion from the pack.*

/~/~/~/~/

Sebastian fully intended to find Madison and drag him down to the restaurant for breakfast, but Lucius found him first. Lucius was a sexy man who showed off his assets with every step he took, but Sebastian was strangely unaffected.

"Sebastian," Lucius was also terminally cheery. "Come to see what the boss man does around here? Is Madison still giving you a hard time?"

"Madison and I are mated," Sebastian said stiffly, following Lucius into the office. Vincent, Lucius's mate was already there, sitting on the couch drinking coffee.

"I thought I saw Madison in the bar earlier," Lucius shook his head. "Not even mating can slow him down, huh? Sucks to be you." He sat next to his mate and slung an arm around Vincent's shoulder. The two men shared a fond look which reminded Sebastian of what he was missing.

"Yes, about that. What the hell is he doing running the place when you're pulling a huge salary to do nothing but sit around and make goo-goo eyes at your mate?"

"Hey, it's the way it is in a pack, man. Don't sweat it," Lucius said with a grin Sebastian itched to wipe off his face. "Look, none of this was intentional. When Damien was running this place, he did a lot of the stuff himself. Scott used to get really upset about it. But when I took over, I'd ask Damien questions about what to do and he always said to ask Madison. I asked Madison and he would get that cute little frown on his face and say he'd take care of it. He's good at it. This place has never run so smoothly."

"And you don't think you're taking advantage?" Sebastian roared. "You have a pack structure designed to protect smaller wolves, and yet you take advantage of them too. Don't think I haven't noticed all the wait staff are subs. Most of the guys in the kitchen are subs. The only big guys in the place working, are the bouncers, the chef, and the bar manager. How is that fair?"

Lucius laughed. "You try getting a Dom to fill those positions. Damien never specified he wanted subs for those jobs, it's just they're the only applications he used to get. The subs like working at the club. The salaries are better than a local fast food chain, they don't have to interact with humans much and they are in the perfect place to attract the eye of a new master. Honestly, you make it sound like we're taking advantage, but you see how you feel when the sub you hired to work the bar comes in four days later with a new Master on his arm who claims he doesn't want him working. It's a freaking nightmare, I tell you."

"Madison doesn't work the bar, or in the kitchen, he runs this freaking place. Yet I bet if I look at his paycheck and compare it to yours I will see a substantial difference."

"Well, yeah, but I take all the responsibility," Lucius said. "If there's a fire, or when your friend flooded the place...."

"Damien, actually no, Scott and Madison dealt with that," Sebastian firmly. "Face it; you're the front of this club, on Damien's behalf, yeah? But who makes sure there's food in the pantry, bottles in the bar, wages are paid, deliveries and supply invoices paid? Who deals with the Dom/sub concerns when they crop up because that's bound to happen with all the egos in this place? Madison's not only doing that, he's also coping with all of the pack stuff Damien and Scott send him every day."

"Hey look," Lucius tried to sound conciliatory, but Sebastian wasn't about to back down. "I am sorry if Madison spent his mating night bitching about the amount of work he does every day, but you can't blame any of us for that. Madison does all this by himself."

"Madison didn't have to say anything, and he wouldn't because he's too fucking loyal," Sebastian growled. "I saw how fucking useless you all were when he was missing; trying to find numbers for suppliers; irate people calling because they hadn't received confirmation of restaurant bookings and shit like that."

"Yeah, well Damien was a mess and you weren't much better and that was when you said you'd never mate him anyway."

"I've claimed him now," Sebastian clenched his fists. "And on the first day of my mating, instead of spending it how you probably spent yours, I woke up to my mate worried about being late for fucking work."

"He always worries," Lucius laughed.

"He shouldn't have to," Sebastian strode across the room and grabbed Lucius by the throat, pulling him away from Vincent who growled but didn't interfere. "My little mate runs this club; runs around after the Alpha keeping the pack happy; basically working himself to the fucking bone and you laugh about his concerns?"

"Get your hands off me," Lucius warned and Sebastian could see the wolf in the man's eyes. "I'm giving you some leniency because you're helping me and Vincent out, but don't think I won't bite you on the ass."

It was Sebastian's turn to laugh. "You and who's army?" he sneered. "I've been playing with hellhounds since before I could walk. I'm the Prince of Death. You think I'm scared of a puppy like you?"

"Let me go," Lucius's face was going red and Vincent stood up.

"Please, let my mate go," Vincent said, a tremor in his voice. The boy wanted to fight, but Sebastian could see he was still only a pup himself. "He didn't mean to make light of your concerns about your mate. Maybe we do tend to joke a bit where Madison is concerned, but he does such a good job we don't want to lose him. Fighting's not the answer. Sitting down and talking is."

"I wouldn't waste my breath fighting with you." Sebastian dropped Lucius on the couch and flexed his shoulders. "But everywhere I go in this club, in this pack, I hear Madison being treated like a king-sized fucking joke. It annoyed me before and it infuriates me now. Do you know how badly he wants to fit in, and you guys just laugh about his worries behind his back? How the fuck is that fair?"

A gasp had Sebastian swirling around. Malacai and Madison were standing there. "Madison." Sebastian closed the space between them and pulled his mate into his arms. "I was just about to come find you and see if we could share brunch."

"We've got a problem," Madison whispered. "Malacai said his wolf wanted to submit to me, and people have been weird around me all morning. Is it because I killed the hellhound?"

"Holy shit." Lucius leaned forward, sniffing. "What the hell's happened to your wolf? *I* want to submit to him and I only submit to Damien."

"See?" Madison's blue eyes implored Sebastian for an answer. An answer he didn't have.

"I don't know what the problem is, sweetness," he said soothingly, holding Madison close. His poor mate was trembling. "But we will sort it out. Maybe your wolf is stronger; these guys won't keep expecting you to do all the jobs around here anymore."

"I like my job," Madison said into his chest.

"I know you do, but getting a pay increase and more respect wouldn't hurt, would it?" Sebastian smiled as Malacai coughed behind him.

"We need to go and see Damien and it has to be at the Pack House," the second explained. "Madison's going to have to shift and he can't do that here. There's something definitely changed about his wolf and that can have implications for his pack position."

"I saw him shifted yesterday," Sebastian said crossly. "There's nothing wrong with him."

"It might be a size thing, something to do with his immortality or killing that Underworld beast yesterday," Malacai said. "We won't know until Madison shifts again."

"I've got to get the supply invoices paid," Madison said fretfully.

"I'll do them," Vincent offered. "You go and do...whatever and Lucius and I will make sure your desk is cleared by the time you get back."

Madison looked like he was going to protest, but Sebastian pulled him away. "They don't know how to do that stuff," Madison whispered as they strode down to the garages, wolves falling over themselves to get out of their way.

"Then maybe it's about time they learned," Sebastian said. His mind was still reeling from what Malacai said. He really needed to talk to his father, but if Thanatos was mate chasing he probably wouldn't respond. The only other person who could help was Hades. Sebastian hoped it didn't come to that. His Uncle could be an unusual man to deal with.

Chapter Seventeen

Madison was a mess; he couldn't think and he could barely walk. After all his years of serving his Alpha as faithfully and as honestly as he knew how, his position in the pack was threatened simply because he'd got involved with men from the Underworld. He shook his head when Sebastian asked if he wanted to take his own car and he didn't say anything as Sebastian helped him into the back of one of the pack SUVs. Malacai took the driver's seat, which Madison expected, but he was surprised when Sebastian climbed in after him, instead of sitting in the front.

"Try not to worry," Sebastian said softly as Madison snuggled under his arm.

"I'm going to lose my pack," Madison whimpered. "I've been here over forty years. I've never once gone against the Alpha or anyone else. I've worked fucking hard all my life and now this...we don't even know what *this* is." He could feel his tears rolling down his face.

"Damien's not like that," Malacai said, from the front of the vehicle. "He's not angry with you. He just wants to make sure none of this is because of what happened when you were captured. That's all."

"How could it be?" Madison said crossly. "Yeah, that asshole drugged me, but he drugged Scott too, and no one's avoiding the Alpha Mate or treating him like he's going to freak out any moment and go on a rampage."

Malacai shook his head but no one said anything else during the trip. Madison alternated between wanting to run as far away as he possibly could from everyone and everything, and getting angry because for whatever reason his mating had turned him into a super freak. He rubbed the spot where his tattoo marked his chest. His wolf loved being marked as mated and so did he. But what if it'd changed him somehow?

By the time the Pack House came into view, his nerves weren't any better. The pack grounds, where children usually played and women sat and gossiped were empty and there were six enforcers on the porch; Damien and Scott standing in the middle of them.

"Great," Madison muttered. "You told Damien I was a fucking killing machine too, I suppose."

"I told him the truth," Malacai looked over the back of his seat. "That my wolf wants to submit to you and believe me, you're not the only one freaked out about this. I'll text Elijah; he's probably going to want to draw some blood so he and Miles can do their thing."

"Let's see if Damien has anything for lunch," Sebastian suggested softly as he got out of the car.

"Oh we won't be fed," Madison followed his mate. "Wolves don't eat with people they might have to kill."

"Well, you're immortal now and I'm quite capable of cooking."

That didn't make Madison feel any better. He approached the steps, feeling nervous about facing his Alpha for the first time in a long time. Damien looked surly as always, but Scott beamed and ran down the steps towards them.

"Madison, you got mated," he said cheerily, crushing Madison in his arms before stepping back. "You've been freaking busy since we saw you last. Not only taming the grouchiest man in history, but I heard something about you killing hellhounds? I didn't know you had it in you."

"It was only one, and it was rogue." Madison shuffled his feet before daring to look at Damien. "Alpha, you wanted to see me?"

"Malacai text me some cock-and-bull story about his wolf wanting to submit to you," Damien sauntered forward. "I had to see it for myself." He moved closer and then stepped back. "Whoa, that's a powerful wolf spirit you got going on there. Are you here to take over the pack?"

"NO!" Madison stamped his foot, his anger winning out against his nerves. Seeing Damien so cautious was the final straw. "How can a piddly-assed wolf like me run a pack? Huh? Huh? I'm damn near a runt, I always have been and now for some mysterious reason, just because I'm mated, everyone's weird around me. I'm still the same person I always was, still hoping for an ounce of fucking respect for all the hard work I do;

still hoping one day someone will fucking accept me the way I am. I've never been a danger to you or anyone in this pack. Never. I gave my loyalty to you over forty years ago. I work my ass off for you and this is the thanks I get. Greeted with fucking enforcers like I'm a fucking rogue? I deserve better than that. I deserve respect, damn it."

He stamped his foot again and then froze as the same howling that accompanied his claiming the night before rang through the air and six huge black hellhounds suddenly appeared in front of the Pack House. Damien pulled Scott behind him, which earned him a thump from his mate. Malacai hurried to his Alpha's side and the six enforcers surrounded Damien and Scott, their faces white.

Madison turned to Sebastian who was smiling. "What the hell just happened? Where did these guys come from?"

"You are a Prince of the Underworld now, and these are your faithful hounds," Sebastian was almost chuckling. "I'm guessing after killing that rogue yesterday and then claiming me, your wolf is now seen as their Alpha. Juno," he nodded to the largest dog, "you favor us with your presence. Come forward and meet your new Prince."

Madison held his ground as the tall, powerful and hellishly freaky looking hound walked towards him. He hadn't paid much attention to the one he killed the day before. Juno was like a giant mastiff, his canine teeth hung over his jaw and his eyes were bright red. But his black fur shone in the sunlight and his muscles rippled with every step. When he was within three feet of Madison, he bowed his head low, his legs almost bent in half.

Trying to think of something profound to say, because it wasn't every day Madison had the opportunity to greet a hellhound, he squeaked when he heard a voice in his head.

Prince of the Underworld, the hounds are at your command. Do you wish us to kill these wolf pups?

"No," Madison yelled and everyone looked at him. "No," he repeated in a softer voice. "I was simply expressing loyalty to my Alpha and things might have gotten a little out of hand. Nothing for you to worry about."

Juno looked over his shoulder at Damien and Scott. Damien looked ready to shift, Scott had a huge smile on his face and when he caught Madison's eye he gave him a quick thumbs up.

That Alpha is older than most of his kind, but no match for us; Juno's voice had an otherworldly charm to it, as it rang through Madison's mind. *However, if you wish them alive, so be it. But think twice before you call him Alpha again. You have ingested the blood of our kind and that of your mate. You rule our kind now. You don't have to show your belly to him anymore.*

"Thank you," Madison whispered, unsure how he felt about the weirdest conversation he'd ever had. "You and your friends can go. I will see you back home, sometime soon."

Juno nodded again and then the air shimmered and rang with the sounds of howls as he and his friends disappeared.

"You handled that very well," Sebastian said proudly.

"I'm not so sure. I think I'm going to faint." Madison felt his legs wobble and then there was nothing but darkness.

Chapter Eighteen

"Are you going to let me into the house or shall I take Madison back to the Underworld?" Sebastian arched his eyebrow at Damien who was glaring at Madison in his arms.

"You're not going anywhere until I know what the hell those...those...things were on my grounds," Damien snarled.

"Well, duh," Scott said with his normal good humor. "They were hellhounds. Didn't the red eyes, drooling fangs, and black fur clue you in? Even I knew that. Come on in, Sebastian. I'll get Madison a glass of water. It sounds like he's had quite a time of it, lately."

"Scott," Damien pulled him back as Sebastian walked past. "This...he...did Madison call those things?"

"They were summoned by his anger," Sebastian said, winking at Scott. "They only come when they're called. So watch your temper around him."

"See...how...what...?" Damien seemed far more shook up about the whole experience than Scott did. Sebastian decided to ignore him until he calmed down. He spotted Elijah sitting in the living room although the small man jumped up when he saw Madison's unconscious state.

"He fainted," Sebastian said quickly. "Scott's just gone to get him some water."

"Should I draw his blood now?" Elijah indicated his bag. "Damien said we needed to take samples from him to find out why he's...wow, so much more powerful than before."

"He's become Alpha of the Hellhounds. I claimed him last night. That's not going to show up in your blood tests." Sebastian carefully laid Madison on the couch and stroked the hair back from his face. Madison's eyelids were already fluttering and by the time Scott came in with a glass of water, he was starting to stir.

"Sebastian," Madison murmured. Sebastian leaned forward and Madison hit him hard across the arm.

"What was that for?" Sebastian resisted the urge to rub his arm although Madison packed quite a punch.

"For not telling me my position came with hellhounds and spooky powers." Madison struggled to sit up. Scott sat at his feet, his face alive with curiosity as he handed over the glass.

"That big one, was he talking to you?"

Madison nodded as he took a couple of gulps of water. "Yeah, some mind connection thing. How did he do that?"

Sebastian found himself the focus of two sets of bright blue eyes and a scowling set of gray ones. He held out his arm and after a moment's hesitation, Madison snuggled into him, still holding his glass.

"The Underworld is a land of myths and legends, like anything connected with death," Sebastian said, resting his arm around Madison's waist. "Half the world has visions of fire and brimstone while other people don't even consider it. But for me and people like my dad and Hades, it's a very real place full of nasties people prefer not to believe in."

"Bet you had an interesting childhood," Scott said. He'd moved so he was sitting at Damien's feet while Malacai had Elijah perched on his lap.

"It was interesting, yep, and it meant as I got older, there was very little that would faze me. It's not a bad place. Quiet for the most part, unless Hades is entertaining, but it has its moments. The hellhounds you saw today are the Underworld enforcers, I suppose you would call them."

"That doesn't explain why they're attached to Madison and why Madison's wolf spirit is ten times stronger than it was last time I saw him. Is he going to turn into one of them?" Sebastian always knew Damien took the safety of his pack seriously, but he didn't like the way Madison flinched under his arm.

"Madison is no different today than he was last week," he said strongly. "And maybe now he's become Alpha of the Hellhounds you guys might start treating him with respect."

"You're their Alpha?" Scott beamed. "That is wicked cool."

"Thank *you* for talking to me, not about me," Madison said. "I'm sitting right here. I'm not deaf and while I haven't got a clue what happened between yesterday and today, except I now have a mate, and became Prince of the Underworld and somehow those hounds like me, I can still speak for myself."

"You're going to need to watch your temper too," Sebastian said quickly. "The hounds are tuned into your emotions. Anger to them means confrontation and as their Alpha, they won't let you face that alone."

"Then you'd better treat me right," Madison snapped. "Or I'll set them on your ass."

Sebastian coughed and covered his mouth with his hand so his mate wouldn't see him smile. "I'll keep that in mind," he said gravely.

"Now see," Damien said angrily, "that right there is my problem with all of this. How do I know you aren't going to call them in on us the next time someone says the wrong thing? I can't have those things around my pack or at the club."

"I didn't call them this time," Madison said softly and Sebastian winced at the pain in his voice. "I sent them away as soon as I knew why they came. I've been loyal to you for over forty years. I took my turn as your sub when you demanded and yes, I pushed for a better position when you callously decided I didn't excite you anymore. I have run around after you, kept you organized, done everything you asked of me because I've always been grateful you gave me a home and a place in your pack despite my size. I've been called frigid, an alpha wannabe, and a drama queen and I've never once complained. Not once."

"We couldn't do without you," Scott said softly.

"Well you'll have to learn," Madison said his voice breaking. "Because now, when you should be happy for me that I've found my true mate after all this time, you've taken the first day of my mated life and shown how little I've meant to you. I'm talking to you, Damien. You've taken all my years of loyalty, all my years of service and shoved them back in my face as meaningless. How could you ever dream in a million years I'd be a danger to this pack? That fucking kills me and it's the final straw. I'm not going to take it anymore. Come on, Sebastian."

"Where we going, hon?" Sebastian glared at Damien, who had the grace to look embarrassed. It didn't help that Scott was also glaring at his mate and Malacai looked worried.

"Anywhere but here."

Sebastian stood, wrapped Madison in his arms and rubbed his tattoo. Seconds later they were in the Underworld, lying on their bed. Sebastian wasn't sure what to do with the crying mate in his arms, so he just held on tight and prayed the storm would pass. He really wasn't good with tears but the creative ways his mind came up with for making Damien pay kept him occupied.

Chapter Nineteen

"Sweetness, you have to eat," Sebastian said gently. "It's been five days and you've barely eaten a thing."

"My wolf is hurting," Madison said listlessly, pushing his plate away. "I've been part of a pack for so long, my wolf side misses it, misses the Alpha. That side of me doesn't understand what we've done wrong and I can't explain it either. I just don't know what I'm going to do."

Sebastian could think of a few things, but they'd been doing those things for five solid days and his dick was too sensitive to consider another round. "Why don't you run with the hounds?" he asked, stumped for new ideas. He'd already taken Madison to see the River Styx and the mountains of Aureus. They'd gone hunting for snakes; Sebastian learned to play video games. He even thought of asking Lasse to transport Madison's car to the Underworld, so he could learn to drive, but there weren't any roads nearby.

"They won't want me either," Madison said. He stood up and Sebastian was shocked with how thin his mate was. "I'm going back to bed."

"No, no you're not," Sebastian said. "I'll call Lasse; we'll get him to take us to see Nereus and his mates in Cloverleah."

"They're not going to like my wolf, any more than Damien does. I won't bring danger to that pack either."

"You're not a danger to anyone," Sebastian was getting desperate. "I can call the hounds; you don't see people scared of me."

"Then they're idiots," Madison smiled, but it was a weak imitation of the vivacious man of a week ago. "Tell Juno I might run with them later. I'm just really tired."

He wandered out of the breakfast nook, his hair uncombed, his pajama bottoms at least three days old. With no makeup and without his suits, Madison looked like a homeless waif and Sebastian's heart ached. He waved his hand, the breakfast dishes cleared away and sat at the table for a long time, wondering if it was possible for an immortal to die of heartbreak. Because without his pack and his refusal to accept the hounds as his own, that seemed like a real possibility for Madison. It was going to take more than sex to keep him alive.

/~/~/~/~/

Madison sat on the bed and stared at his phone. There were dozens of messages – Scott, Malacai, and Elijah all begging him to come back. John and Boris also sent messages of complaint after

258

complaint about how nothing was getting done, but there was nothing from Damien. Throwing his phone on the bedside table, Madison flung himself back on the bed, his eyes fixed on the ceiling. He knew he wasn't being a good mate to Sebastian. They had sex frequently and while Sebastian could make his body sing with a few well-placed strokes of his fingers, Madison's heart wasn't in it. He was sure it was only because of their mating pull that he could get hard at all and that was no reflection on Sebastian's skill. It was just with his wolf the way he was, and his own mind, he admitted to himself, sex was the last thing he needed.

Admittedly it wasn't all about sex. Sebastian had been a font of patience, listening to him ranting one minute and crying the next. But Sebastian couldn't offer any solutions and if Madison was honest, he was getting sick of his whiny self, too.

Sebastian doesn't deserve this, he thought. *All my life I've wanted a mate and look what happens when I get one. I do nothing but cry and moan about shit out of our control. No wonder he wants sex so often. It's the only way to shut me up.*

Madison knew he was bordering on depression. It wasn't so much him, as his wolf. He was hurting, yes. After all he'd done for the pack and Damien in particular, the man proved he'd never really trusted him. And yet, for the longest time, he'd given Damien his all. He wondered if he'd ever stop hurting about it, but figured probably not. He still got upset at times, over being ejected from his father's pack and that was so long ago he couldn't remember what his father looked like.

Thinking back to those days when he was young, Madison

remembered the strength he dredged up just to keep going after his father beat him. He was a lone wolf for three years before he heard about Damien's pack. Specifically, a pack where gay wolves were welcome and no questions asked. Bumming around the streets of Washington State at the time, he hitched, begged rides and walked from Olympia to San Antonio. It took him four months, but when he finally found Damien's club, the man took him in without hesitation. He was fed, clothed and started working as soon as he was well enough to show his thanks. He'd never stopped.

"Well, that's over now," Madison told the ceiling. "Time for a new plan; at least I have a mate this time."

He looked down at his shabby pajamas and ran a finger through his hair. He was disgusted with himself. All the beautiful clothes

Thanatos had given him and he couldn't even be bothered to get dressed. "This is not who I am," he told himself sternly and climbed off the bed.

"Sebastian!" he yelled as he started going through his closet.

"What is it? Is everything okay?" Sebastian's head appeared around the door, worry etched around his eyes.

"No it's not okay, but I will be," Madison said pulling a beautiful dark gray suit from the rack and laying it on the bed. "Can you call Lasse and find a way to get my car out of the garage under the club. You said we could go traveling and it's about time you learned to drive. I'll pack our bags. We'll go wherever the roads take us. I hope you've got plenty of money because I refuse to stay in rat-infested hotels."

"We can stay wherever you want," Sebastian grinned. "It's good to have you back, sweetness."

Madison didn't bother to reply. The mirror told him his hair was a disgrace. He needed to do serious damage control on his ends and his skin...when was the last time he moisturized? Damn, he had some work to do.

Chapter Twenty

Back in San Antonio

"Am I the Alpha here or not?" Damien demanded. He was sitting in his office, his desk littered with papers. The evening crowd was already building in the club below yet Damien didn't have a minute to enjoy himself.

"That's the rumor," Malacai said, completely unruffled. "But I told you, I'm not running all over town looking for whiskey that should have been ordered three days ago. Elijah is expecting me home; get one of the enforcers to do it."

"I can't," Damien slammed his fist on the desk. "Scott won't come to the club so that means six of the enforcers have to stay on pack grounds. Two more are on bouncer duty and the other two were apparently rostered for vacations nobody bothered to tell me about."

"Lucius knows the supplier, doesn't he? Get him and Vincent to take a quick trip."

"They're on their way to fucking Denver, Vincent's home pack. Fucking men bowing down to their mates on every single little thing. '*I promised Vincent a trip and I can't let him down now*,'" Damien's impersonation of Lucius's excuses wasn't that good but he was beyond caring.

"Well, at least he has his mate with him," Malacai said pointedly as he stood up. "And I'm going home to mine. Until you get off your high horse and get Madison back, I guess you'll be busy in your office all by your lonesome."

"Get out," Damien snarled. The slam of the door did nothing to appease his temper. He looked at the pile of papers, and then at his phone. Nothing from Scott, not even a text and Damien knew if he made the run out to the Pack

House he'd be greeted with a locked bedroom door. Scott made his position crystal clear. Until he apologized to Madison and got the PA to come back, he was persona non grata.

His office door opened and Boris stormed in. "This meat is shit. It stinks. Madison wouldn't have allowed this. Fix it, or I go." He slammed a platter of steaks on the desk and stormed out.

"Fuck!" Damien yelled. He was horny, miserable, up to his eyeballs in work he didn't even know he had to do and now his papers were covered in blood splatter.

"Alpha," John the bar manager looked uneasy as he peered in the door. "None of the bartenders turned up tonight and we've got a party of twenty in, plus our regular guests. What should I do?"

"Call some of the subs on the roster and tell them they'll get bonuses if they can get here in fifteen minutes," Damien snapped.

"I tried that, but they won't come in. None of them have been paid this week."

"What do you mean they haven't been paid?" Damien was stunned.

John shuffled in, tilting his head. He dragged a pile of papers out from the mess on the desk. "The timesheets were put in three days ago, as per usual. You said you wanted them on your desk and that you'd handle it."

"I'll pay them in cash, last week's and this week's pay, just get them in."

"Yes, Alpha," John bobbed his head as he backed out the door.

"Who else hasn't been paid?" Damien muttered as he threw the meat platter on the floor and hunted through his papers. Supply accounts, requisition orders, rosters submitted for approval. Timesheets; fuck there was at least thirty of them and none of them paid. At least he'd have the cash because the banking was sitting in a bin under his desk. He hadn't had time to do that either.

"Boss," Ron, one of the enforcers stuck his head around the door. "We've got a problem in one of the back rooms. A sub's crying, the Dom's yelling loud enough for the bar patrons to hear. What do you want me to do?"

"What do you usually do when this happens?" Damien was going to be bald if this went on much longer.

Ron looked at the floor. "Well, usually we'd call Madison and he'd talk to the sub, and he was pretty good at calming down the Doms as well."

"Is there anything that man didn't do?"

"Not much," Ron said. "So, are you coming...or...?"

"Call in the Alpha Mate, he's better at this sort of thing than me," Damien ordered. Scott couldn't resist a crying sub, and then maybe Damien would get a chance to see him.

"Tried that already, boss. He said no. Said, and I quote, 'you got yourself into this fucking mess, you get yourself out,' his words, not mine," Ron added hastily.

"Double crap on a crap stick," Damien ran his hands over his face. "Okay, I'm coming." The truth of it was Damien didn't want to set foot in the club because the moment he did, he had to field a dozen complaints coming from all sides. He strode through his club determined not to look at anyone, or give anyone the chance to stop him. Crying sub, then wages, then...he groaned at the thought of his long to-do list. All he wanted to do was be at home in the Pack House with his mate curled up in his arms. A mate who was getting frostier with every minute Damien spent at the club. *How the hell did I cope with all this before I was mated?*

You had Madison, his brain supplied helpfully.

/~/~/~/~/

"Let me in," Damien roared as he banged on his bedroom door. After a hellishly long night, trying to catch up on the monumental list of things that still needed doing; fielding complaints from pack members right and left; at around three in the morning, he decided he'd had enough and left the club. He didn't care if the wretched place burned to the ground. He hadn't held or spoken to Scott since their last argument the day Madison left.

He wanted his mate and he wasn't going to let a fucking thing like a locked door stop him anymore.

"I swear if you don't open this door, Scott, I'm going to rip it off its hinges. I'm warning you, I am not in the mood to put up with your nonsense." He pounded on the door again, his fist cracking one of the panels.

"Nonsense?" Scott wrenched the door open. With the sudden rush of his mate's scent, Damien's tiredness and frustration disappeared. His cock hardened to the point of pain and all he could think of was slamming his mate up against the nearest wall and pounding into his body. So intent on his plan, he barely noticed the right hook Scott threw until it landed.

"What the fuck?" Damien rubbed his jaw line.

"You call standing up for my friend nonsense?" Scott was furious, Damien could smell it and that's without the stern face and strong hands planted on his hips. His naked hips. Oh fuck...Damien wanted so bad. "All you had to do was make one phone call, send one little text and all your problems would be solved. Madison has loved you and looked up to you for longer than I've been alive. He didn't deserve to be made to feel like he wasn't trusted."

"You saw those hounds, you've heard the stories. They could rip this pack apart without a second thought and there's nothing you or I could do about it. For fuck's sake, this isn't just about you and me. I've got the whole pack to think about." Oh shit, Damien knew as soon as he shut his mouth, he'd made a mistake. It was his cock's fault; Damien would swear that to his dying day. He was normally more careful about how he phrased things with his mate. The way Scott's eyes narrowed and his usually full lips tightened, Damien prepared himself for a blast.

"And you don't think I care about the welfare of this pack? I'm Alpha Mate, in case you've forgotten. Who is it who stays here and listens to your pack mates' concerns? You can't be bothered and someone has to, or have you forgotten the mess going on here when I first arrived?"

No, Damien would never forget the fire, the stolen children and the abuses he found out about in the pack when he and Scott mated. He'd been horrified that he'd let so much go on behind his back while he'd played lord of the manor at his club. It'd been his darkest moment and without Scott, he'd have never gotten through it.

"Do you want me to sell the club, is that it? Because I can, just say the word." The club was Damien's baby; he'd built it from the ground up. But Damien was getting desperate. He was unraveling and with the state things were in, soon he wouldn't have a club to enjoy.

"What will all your Doms and subs do if you sell the place? They make up over half the pack. Where will they find their safe place? Are you going to tell them they should work at other clubs, find employment elsewhere? You'd trust humans to ensure our precious shifters are treated right in unfamiliar surroundings when they want to play?"

Damien pulled his hair in frustration. "You know I don't want that, but look at us. I've got no one at the club, things are going to shit. You're supposed to be helping me, not locking your door against me every night because of one little pack member."

"That one little pack member as you so scathingly put it, kept your life running smooth and your club running sweet. So, Madison can call the hellhounds? So what? You saw they left as soon as he told them to, he's their alpha. They listen to him. And you know what I think?" Scott stepped closer and Damien moaned as a fresh wave of his mate's scent hit him.

"I think you're scared," Scott said in a low voice. "You've always been the strongest wolf and have relied on your strength to keep this pack safe. But sometimes, you don't have to be the strongest; you need to be the smartest."

"What do you mean?" Damien hoped his mate wasn't implying he was stupid.

"It means, take a lesson from Cloverleah. Kane's not the strongest in that pack; hell, he isn't even the strongest wolf. Matthew, Jax, and Anton, even Griff could take out Kane in a heartbeat. But he's surrounded himself with strength. All the men in the pack would willingly die for him, and he for them. He trusts them all and they're loyal to him. Do you understand what I'm saying?"

"This is about trusting Madison?" Damien's heart and cock leaped in tandem as Scott took a step closer, nodding his head.

"I should have trusted that Madison has never let me down, has always been loyal to me and this pack and that even though he can command the hounds from hell, I should see that as a bonus to pack security?" Damien was winging it. His body trembled at the thought of Scott in his arms.

"You're getting warmer," Scott took another step closer.

"I need to apologize to him, let him know how much I appreciate him and his mate's offer about running the club. I'll increase his salary, stand before the pack and let them know he speaks for me in the club and then when I've fixed that problem, I will come back home and spend all my time loving on my mate who is so much wiser than I am?"

"Bingo." Scott's arms were warm around Damien's waist, his body comforting and arousing all in one go. Damien felt his body slump for the first time in five days. "See, it wasn't that hard, was it? Admitting I was right?"

"If it means my cock will get some attention, I'll tell you you're right every freaking day," Damien growled.

"Aww and I thought you'd be happy with a cuddle," Scott teased. But his head was turned up and Damien was quick to accept the invitation. Five days without his mate in his arms had been torture and he wasn't going to go another second without tasting his mate's lips. He'd make the call to Madison in the morning...or maybe the afternoon. He had a lot of catching up to do with his mate first.

Chapter Twenty-One

"Whew, that was great fun, want to do it again?" Madison's face was flushed with excitement as they stepped off the Steel Eel ride. Sebastian suggested before leaving town, Madison should see the sorts of treats offered in San Antonio and took him to SeaWorld. He was seriously second-guessing his decision. He and heights did not agree.

"Can we sit down for a moment? On something that won't move this time," he suggested quietly.

"We could go and see the alligators again." Madison bounced in his new sneakers. Seeing him in jeans and a polo shirt was a bit of an adjustment, but Madison happily complied when he'd said suits would be uncomfortable if they wanted to have any fun.

"I think you scared them enough, last time," Sebastian managed a shaky laugh. "Come on. I'm older than you. I need to sit down for a minute."

"You're only as old as the man you feel," Madison whispered as he trotted along, his head turning from side to side as he took in all the attractions. "I can't believe I didn't know this place was here," he said. He shook his head, chuckling, as Sebastian found an empty bench and collapsed on it with a sigh. It was going to take a while for his knees to function properly.

"I guess it's got to do with work/life balance," Sebastian said making sure their shoulders were touching when Madison sat beside him. "You've worked hard for a long time. Now it's time for some fun. You could have warned me you were an adrenaline junkie, though."

"I didn't know these things could be so much fun. I want to try the

Great White next," Madison bounced in his seat at the idea. Sebastian suppressed a shudder.

"Your phone's been ringing all afternoon. Are you going to answer it anytime soon?" He said, hoping to provide a distraction but when Madison's face dropped, he wished he'd kept his big mouth shut.

"It's Damien," Madison sighed.

Sebastian was puzzled. "I thought you wanted him to call you." During their confinement in the Underworld, Madison alternated between raging and crying because the big alpha *hadn't* called him.

"I did, but I don't know what he's going to say and I don't think my wolf could take any more hurt," Madison whispered but Sebastian still looked around to make sure no one was listening.

"He's probably calling to beg you to come back. That club will be falling apart without you."

Madison snorted. "Damien thinks he can handle anything, but I know Scott's been giving him a hard time about me. That's probably why he's calling. But we've got a plan. We're going to travel, see more of these amazing places. I bet there are roller coasters like the Steel Eel all over the country. We can ride them all."

Sebastian gulped, glancing up at the huge steel monstrosity. The screaming was hurting his ears. He had no doubt his little mate would find them all, and privately, Sebastian didn't think he'd be able to cope. One day in a theme park was more than enough. "You miss your friends, sweetness," he said in a low voice. "That's understandable. You've been loyal to Damien all this time. It's not like you to ignore him now."

"I'm not being disloyal," Madison said, his head down. "It's just, what if he does want me back.

Things won't have changed. I'll still be working 24/7 with no recognition, no appreciation. My wages barely keep me in clothes and hair products. I can't get ahead if I keep working there and you said yourself, I get no respect."

"You're in a position to create changes," Sebastian said, risking entwining his little finger with Madison's. "If he wants you back, you can demand your position be given more respect, more money, whatever you want. Negotiate time off at the very least. Tell him you want an assistant, or even better, two of them. Damien can afford it."

"My own assistants?" Madison looked intrigued by the idea so Sebastian pushed on.

"Why not? You have an important job and you should get that recognized too. With assistants, you can have regular time off, coinciding with my own, of course.

But think about it. You are in the driver's seat with this. You can pretty much demand anything and I bet Damien would agree. If Scott's giving him a hard time, he'll want to smooth things over on the home front and he can't do that if he's working at the club."

"I never stopped to think how all this stopped you from getting your own job there."

"Meh, I was only taking it to be with you. But now you're a little more," Sebastian looked around. No one was paying them any attention. "Powerful," he whispered, "I'm sure a lot of the club Doms will stop giving you grief as well. You could have a lot of fun with this. Think about the alligators and how quickly they swam away when they scented you."

"It was funny," Madison agreed, nodding his head. "And that attendant's face; he'd never seen anything like it before."

"Being one of us has its perks and you can have some fun with your newfound power. But look, you have choices." Sebastian swallowed again. He could see his future filled with roller coasters, him screaming all the way with a laughing Madison by his side. The laughing Madison would be a blessing but he wasn't sure his nerves could stand the rest of it. With the right conditions, working at the club was a better choice.

"We never have to worry about money. You don't have to work. You can go back to just being a pack member if that's what you want. We can travel, if you prefer. Or you can be the man I know you are, and you can march back into Damien's life and dictate your terms, not his. Whatever you want, I'll support you."

"We still don't know he wants me back," Madison said. "He might have lost the stapler or something.

It would be just like him to think I'm pining in my room and that he can call me about trivial things any time he likes."

Sebastian didn't bother to mention that's exactly what Madison had been doing. He nodded to his mate's pocket as a familiar ring tone started up. "That will be him now, why don't you answer it and see for yourself."

With a noticeable gulp, Madison slipped his phone out of his pocket and tapped the screen. "Yes, Damien?" he asked in a strong voice. Sebastian leaned back on the bench, praying his relief didn't show as he listened to Madison make an appointment for dinner at the club later that evening. *No more roller coasters.*

/~/~/~/

Madison dithered over his clothing choices, a finely cut suit in one hand, his leather pants in the other. The suit would give him more confidence, especially if he teamed it with his jeweled tie. But it would also send the message that he'd made an effort and was eager to work. The leather pants...hmm...with a sigh, he put the suit back in the closet and rifled through his shirts looking for something that went with his eyes and didn't scream "I'm desperate."

"If you don't put something on, we won't be going anywhere," Sebastian said as he came out of the bathroom, toweling his hair. He was already dressed in his typical black camo pants and a black button-down shirt. Madison quickly slipped on his pants before his mate acted on the ideas he could see brewing in those dark eyes. He was already nervous and while sex would be an enjoyable way to spend the evening now he wasn't feeling so blue, he hated being late.

"Did Dad leave the portal to the club, do you know?" he asked as he pulled a blue Eton shirt over his shoulders.

"I haven't seen Dad, although his wing of the house is blocked so I'm assuming he's bonding with his mate. He wouldn't imagine you'd be having problems at the club, so I don't see why he would close it."

"I hope he and Cody are all right," Madison smoothed his shirt, then checked his hair in the mirror. "Cody has a lot of issues; you'd better be nice to him when you meet him."

"Dad will have my guts for garters if I wasn't," Sebastian said soothingly. "Now come on, you look amazing and if we don't move away from this bed you'll be very, very late."

"Can I have a rain check?" Madison stood on tiptoes and kissed Sebastian's chin.

"Always," Sebastian bent over and what was an initial brush of lips quickly turned into a heated kiss. Yes, Madison was nervous about the upcoming meeting, but his day with Sebastian had been truly special and he wanted his mate to know how much he appreciated it. They were both breathing heavily when they finally broke apart.

"Dinner, then bed," Madison said, aware his cheeks were flaming.

"Agreed. Now, where did Dad put this portal of yours?"

/~/~/~/~/

Appearing in the upstairs portion of the club as they did, Madison could see firsthand, things weren't running as smoothly as they usually did as he and Sebastian made their way downstairs. The bar didn't look fully stocked, there wasn't many staff on duty and the relief on Malacai's face when he saw them couldn't be faked.

"I'm so glad you came," he said rushing forward and actually shaking Madison's hand. "Damien's had me on look out for you. We weren't quite sure how you'd get here. He and Scott are waiting in the restaurant."

"They're still talking to one another then?" Madison asked as his eyes scanned the bar, his fingers itching for his tablet.

"Only just," Malacai said. "And only after the boss man promised to call you. He's been pulling his hair out for days."

Madison didn't think it was nice to smirk, but he did it anyway. He nodded to a few familiar faces; Doms who scurried out of his way as he passed. Sebastian chuckled too. It was the alligators all over again.

Damien and Scott were sitting at their usual table. Scott got up as soon as he saw them, hurrying over and enfolding Madison in a huge hug. "Please don't leave again," he whispered before pulling back and saying in his normal voice, "it's great to see you both, come and sit down."

Madison was pleased Scott was his normal friendly self, but it was Damien's reaction he was waiting for. The big Alpha stood as they approached the table, holding out his hand. Surprised, Madison shook it and then let Sebastian help him into his chair.

"Now, if we can have a meal without you two lugs wrecking the furniture, that would be lovely," Scott said as he took his seat next to Damien. Madison saw Sebastian and Damien share a look but neither of them promised anything. He made a mental note to ask about their source of antagonism later when he and his mate were alone.

Traditionally, wolf shifters didn't talk business when they were eating. But Madison barely sat down when Boris came hurrying out of the kitchen, holding out his hands in greeting and wait...was that a smile on his face? Madison didn't think he'd ever seen the gruff man smile.

"Madison, my Madison, I am so pleased you are here. You have come back to stay, yes?"

"We've still got things to discuss," Madison said cautiously, looking at Damien who was glaring while Scott smirked behind his hand.

"Whatever you want, the boss, he'll give it to you," Boris said emphatically. "No matter what, he will give it to you. I told him if you no come back then I walk; buying me stinky meat, pah." Boris returned Damien's glare before he stormed off to the kitchen.

"Stinky meat?" Sebastian asked. "Is it safe to eat here anymore?"

"Of course, it is," Damien growled. "It's just, it's been hectic around here lately, that's all."

Scott thumped Damien on the arm. "Tell them the truth. Running out of alcohol, not checking the meat supplies, bartenders not turning up for work because they hadn't been paid, restaurant reservations unconfirmed, subs needing therapy because no one can calm them down and some of them are refusing to play with any of the Doms until they know Madison is around because he listens to them if they have complaints."

"I've only been gone six days," Madison said quietly. "What happened? I have a system; it's all on my tablet. Dates, times, schedules, when things need to be done. It's all there."

Damien mumbled something.

"Sorry, what was that?" Sebastian said with a smirk. "I didn't hear you."

"I don't know how to use the tablet," Damien met Sebastian's eyes his mouth pulled down. "I never had to use it before."

"That's because Madison did it for you," Scott said, putting his hand on Damien's arm.

Madison also tugged on Sebastian's arm, breaking the two bigger men's staring contest. "Let's enjoy our meal, shall we?" He said smiling up at his mate.

"I'm enjoying it already, and the food hasn't even arrived," Sebastian said with a wink. Damien growled and Scott laughed and Madison felt a lot better about how the evening was going to go.

Chapter Twenty-Two

"Did you see Damien's face when I told him I needed two assistants? I thought he was going to have a coronary." Madison laughed as he threw himself on the bed fully clothed. Sebastian found he loved seeing this side of his mate. The happy confident man had been missing for almost a week. It was great to see him back.

"You got a new job title too, plus a long weekend off every second week, a six-figure salary and four weeks paid leave a year," he reminded, removing his shirt.

"And what a fabulous title it is: Madison Worthington, Chief Operating Officer; second only to you, Mr. CEO of Damien Incorporated." Madison rolled over and Sebastian felt the heat of his stare. "I find I don't have a problem being under you," he added in a lower tone.

"I find I don't have a problem with that either," Sebastian flicked open the button of his pants and they fell to the ground. "But I still think it's something we need to practice." He stepped out of his pants and stalked over to the bed, pleased when the blue in Madison's eyes deepened. "Do you need help getting undressed?"

"I think you should do it," Madison teased, although he toed off his boots and kicked them off the other side of the bed. "Take me, I'm yours," he said with a flourish as he opened his arms wide.

Sebastian didn't need a second invitation. He pounced and quickly found himself with an armful of wriggling mate which was a surprise he found he liked. The past five days, there'd been something decidedly lacking in the bedroom department and as he ravaged Madison's eager mouth, he realized what it was.

Enthusiasm, passion, and dare he think it...affection.

Madison met every thrust of his tongue with a full body thrust. He moaned, whimpered and submitted beautifully as Sebastian stripped off his clothes and bent to nibble and lick every inch of skin he could reach. Sebastian's passion went from "yeah I need a fuck," to "my gods, this man is everything to me; I have to possess him now."

He quickly flipped Madison onto his front and was instantly presented with a stunning ass wiggling enticingly. He'd never rimmed a guy before, but now he couldn't think of anything else. With a sense of wonder, he carefully palmed open Madison's butt cheeks, a tiny pink hole filling his gaze. *Just one lick,* he thought and he bent his head, moaning as Madison's scent filled his nose. He wasn't a shifter, he didn't rely on his nose, but when it was buried in

Madison's most intimate place he wished he had an animal side. Madison smelled of musk and man and yet there was a hint of sweetness that had his tongue flicking out, seeking more.

"Oh my gods," Madison yelled. "No one...wow...fuck...what are you...don't stop."

Sebastian grinned. With their histories, a first he could share with his mate was a bonus. He licked his mate's tight little muscles feeling them tense and then relax under his attentions. Slipping a hand through Madison's parted legs, he lightly stroked the erection he found, teasing his mate's balls while his tongue kept lashing at his ass until he could nudge it inside.

Madison screamed. "Oh please, now, it has to be now. Fuck me!"

Moving quickly, Sebastian found the lube, slathering his cock and pushing some deep inside his mate.

"I can take it," Madison groaned. "Get your cock in there, now."

Lining up, Sebastian took a deep inhale and then pushed as he slowly breathed out. Madison's body welcomed him like it always had, but with the lack of prep, the grip around his cock was tighter and he curbed his urge to rut in deep and carefully edged in and out, taking his time. They were both panting heavily by the time his balls hit Madison's butt.

He leaned over Madison's lightly muscled back, their sweat causing his skin to slide. "You are beautiful, do you know that?" He whispered in Madison's ear.

"I know I'm about to call the hellhounds to bite your ass if you don't move."

Chuckling, Sebastian wrapped his arm around Madison's chest and gently rocked his hips, Madison's groans increasing in volume as he slowly increased his speed. *This means something...special...love...it is.* Sebastian's heart opened and he welcomed the warmth, caring, and compassion that had been missing from his life for so long. His feelings grew until they escaped his body, swirling in the air around them and he felt he had to, he needed to say something.

"Madison," he whispered.

"I know, I can feel it," Madison groaned, "I love you too; now for the love of god will you please touch my dick."

Probably the wrong time to say something if I was looking for a romantic response, Sebastian thought as he did as instructed. Gripping Madison's slender cock he used his mate's juices to slick his palm; Madison rocking into his hand and then back onto his cock. It didn't take long, not with those feelings thickening in the air and Madison slamming back onto him in increasingly faster thrusts. Sebastian felt the stirring in his gut, the spike up his spine and the throb in his balls. He held off, determined they would come together, but when Madison threw his head back and yelled "Love you, Sebastian," he grunted and thrust in deep, holding firm as his cock jerked with his release.

"Love you too, Madison," he whispered against his mate's back. "Love you so much."

"Good," Madison mumbled, "I'll be all mushy with you later, I promise. Now do your magic hand thingy to clean us up then cuddle me close. We have to get up for work in the morning."

Why do I put up with this again...oh yeah, because I love him? With a wave of his hand, Sebastian cleaned them and the bed and then pulled his mate into his arms.

Madison settled with a sigh, his hair tickling his chest and within seconds, faint snores came from his mouth. Sebastian smirked. His mate was regimented in all things, but the ease with which Madison was happy to involve him soothed his heart and quite a few wounds as well. Closing his eyes, Sebastian fell into a dreamless sleep.

Chapter Twenty-Three

Madison hummed as he strolled along the corridor towards the office he now shared with Sebastian. It hadn't taken him long to get the club squared away with suppliers, customers, and staff. Now a month into his new position, he just wished he'd been able to find the new assistants he wanted. Many of the subs hadn't been to college because of their heartbreaking backgrounds and Doms didn't want to work with him. Hopefully, his next applicant was waiting in their office. He apparently had a college degree in business management.

He opened the door, the smile on his face quickly slipping as he took in the scene. Sebastian backed into a corner, a rabid sub, probably the job applicant, trying to get his pants undone. Sebastian's face was a mask of relief as he saw Madison stalk into the room. "Hey, sweetness. Seems this guy has the wrong idea about the job."

"He definitely has," Madison fumed as he recognized the butterfly tattoo on the man's shoulder. "Toby get off your knees, you arrogant pup; what the hell do you think you're doing?"

"I told you, I'd have him one way or another. I'm just showing him what a good assistant I can be, seeing as you clearly can't do the job." Toby smirked as he stood up, running his hands down his naked torso.

"We haven't seen much of each other lately, have we Toby," Madison moved closer. "I seem to recall you took a human master, much to Damien's disgust and left the club. Didn't take you long to come crawling back with your tail between your legs, did it?"

"I like trying new things," Toby said, just as cocky as ever. "Better than being a frigid stick in the mud like you."

Madison looked over his head at Sebastian who winked at him. He'd promised Damien he wouldn't bring the hounds to the club because of the humans around, but that didn't mean he couldn't use his new alpha voice.

"Come here, Toby," he said, his voice deepening with his new power.

Toby's eyes widened in shock and his face went white as his feet moved woodenly in Madison's direction. "What magic is this?"

"Do you know who this man is?" Madison pointed in the direction of his mate.

"He's a friend of the Alpha, and now runs the club." Toby's voice lost all its earlier bravado and he repeated the words like a robot; his body shaking and sweat dotting his brow.

"This is Sebastian D'Eath, son of Thanatos, who is Death himself. Do you know his other claim to fame?"

Toby shook his head.

"He's my mate," Madison voice deepened and sounded like it came from the bowels of the earth. Toby fell, his legs unable to hold him upright.

"I just wanted a job. Malacai said the boss was looking for an assistant, I have the qualifications," Toby's voice rose on a wail.

"Do you?" Madison was surprised, but then he'd always hoped there was more to Toby than being a man-whore. "What qualifications are they?" He stepped over Toby's body and moved into Sebastian's arms. "Miss me?" He asked with a grin.

"Always," Sebastian assured him, walking him over to their chair. "What are you going to do about him?" He nodded to Toby who'd half sat up but was still looking like he'd crapped himself.

"Interview him," Madison said, looking back at Toby. "Go and dress properly for this interview, and be back here in ten minutes. You'll need a shower. Bring any evidence you have of these qualifications you claim to have and if you think you can work for me with your clothes on, prove it."

Toby bobbed his head and scuttled out of the door. "Leave it open," Madison yelled waving a hand in front of his face. "Damn pup, that's got to be the third person this week."

"Fourth." Sebastian laughed. "Remember that sneaky cat shifter who wanted to interview as a professional Dom?"

"Hmm, and thought he could try out his skills on me. I remember," Madison said drily, but then he grinned. "It's fun, though. Not as much as the alligators, but I get my work done a lot quicker these days. No one seems to give me any grief anymore."

Sebastian looked at his tablet. Madison insisted he get one and picked it out personally. "I see from our schedule we have this interview to conduct and then four blissful days off. What did you have planned?"

Madison grinned. His mate knew him so well, and he also knew how lucky he was that Sebastian didn't seem to mind that he liked to schedule activities on their time off, too. He couldn't explain it, it was just the way he was and Sebastian quickly caught on that while a surprise once in a while was fine, as a rule, Madison liked to know what was happening in his day. "Dad wants to take us and Cody to dinner tomorrow night. He didn't say where, but he did say dress nice, so I guess I will be pulling out my jeweled tie again and you'll have to have your suit pressed. Nereus and his mates are coming on Sunday for the day."

"That will be a jeans and boots day," Sebastian said. "He'll probably want to take us somewhere too, but it will be a lot more casual knowing Nereus. It will be good to meet Teilo and see Raff again. I promise to be nice to him," he added.

"You'd better be," Madison said firmly. "Raff promised to leave the puppies with Luke, so we won't have to worry about Killer challenging Juno for his position." He smirked.

"I know that look," Sebastian said cautiously. "You've planned us some time to ourselves, haven't you? I want one day where I don't have to be jarred awake by that fucking alarm. Breakfast in bed, and maybe lunch as well? A full day naked." Madison felt a warm hand cupping his cock and he groaned.

"That's Monday," he said, moving his head back as Sebastian nibbled up his throat.

"Hmm, Friday dinner plans, Sunday friends, Monday bed." Sebastian moved his head away and tilted Madison's face to meet his. "What are we doing on Saturday?"

"Our going out day. There's this awesome place, not far at all, just out on the I-10."

"What's this place called?" Madison wondered if he should keep his mate in suspense, but then his own happiness bubbled over and he reached for his tablet. "It's called Six Flags Fiesta." He scrolled through his pages and then held it up for Sebastian to see.

"It has roller coasters." Sebastian didn't sound as excited as Madison thought he would be.

"Goliath, Batman, Poltergeist; heaps of them all in the one place. Isn't it great? I already ordered passes and get this, we don't even have to wait in line. I ordered us passes for everything. We can ride on these things all day!"

Sebastian shook his head. "Do you realize how much I love you?"

"Of course, and I love you too." Madison wondered why Sebastian brought it up. He wasn't usually romantic, especially in the office.

"I'll agree to this Six Flags Place, on the condition that on our next weekend off, you let me plan what we'll be doing."

Madison pouted. "I thought we had an agreement, one day family, one day friends, one lazy day for us and one day where we went out and did something different."

"I'll stick to the plan," Sebastian promised, "but if you're going to insist I ride roller coasters for a full day this weekend, then I'm going to insist you teach me how to drive. There are lots of exciting things to do in Texas and they don't all have to involve my ass being fifty feet off the ground in some wretched cage contraption."

Madison didn't see anything wrong with riding roller coasters. Sebastian grumbled a bit, but it wasn't as though Madison forced him to go and when he was on them he never screamed or anything. In fact, Sebastian's face was like a rock most times they went and as he was like that ninety percent of the time in the club as well, Madison assumed he didn't have a problem with them. After all, every ride was completely safe; Madison checked the company's safety records before he planned anything involving his beloved Sebastian. He was going to ask what sorts of things Sebastian considered fun, but just then Toby knocked on the door. He looked a lot better fully dressed. Slipping off his mate's knee, Madison sat in his own chair and pulled up his interview questionnaire on his tablet.

"Now, Toby," he said, "Tell me what skills you have that will benefit the running of this club."

Chapter Twenty-Four

Sebastian sat on the bed he now shared with his mate, staring at the dagger Alexander had given him centuries before. He found it hard to recall the lines of Alexander's face. He wracked his brains searching for the good times his heart told him they shared. He remembered them fighting side by side; he remembered the rushed joining of their bodies when they could steal moments away from the others who crowded Alexander continually. He could recall shared jokes, inside things that meant something to them both, but not to the crowds who hung on Alexander's every word. They had a bond, he remembered that, but knowing what he did now, he knew they didn't share the love that came with a mate. Friends, definitely, but not mates.

"You okay?" Madison strolled in from the bathroom, a towel

wrapped around his waist, while he used another one to dry his hair. "You look upset about something."

"I was trying to remember Alexander," Sebastian said and then he looked up to see Madison scowling. "I'm not unhappy with you; I love you, I truly do. I don't miss him...I just...." He trailed off as Madison abandoned his hair and came and sat by his side.

"Was this a gift from him?" Madison pointed to the dagger but didn't touch it.

"His kiss-off gift when he told me he was in love with Bagoas," Sebastian said. He turned to his mate, knowing he had to confess. If he didn't, his guilt would come between them, wrecking everything they'd built so far. "I was holding this knife after Scott came back and told me they'd tried to save you but that Larson asshole moved you again. I sat in that room in the club, trying to get up the nerve to contact my dad. I knew he could save you, you see. I knew that he'd know where you were. He couldn't interfere with Scott, but he could have saved you."

"He saved me anyway," Madison frowned. "I don't understand what the problem is."

"The problem is I had nothing to do with that. Dad did it on his own accord, or the Fates told him to, or something, I don't know. But I sat above the club like a coward, pining for a man who never loved me the way you do. Alexander and I were closer than friends, but when Bagoas came along he had no problem giving his heart to the one it belonged to. I was the one who hung on to something that didn't exist for centuries, hating my dad, hurting you. I could have saved you, don't you see, and I didn't. Because of this!" Sebastian threw the dagger hard against the wall where it dug in with a resounding thwack.

"That's probably not the best way to treat a priceless antique," Madison said. "A museum would kill to have something like that in their collection."

"I don't want to talk about the wretched knife, I'm talking about us," Sebastian implored. "The horror you went through when you were kidnapped; a kidnapping that only happened because of my harsh words; my rejection of you. I could have saved you a lot sooner. Aren't you angry about that?"

"I can be if you want me to be," Madison said calmly. "But I don't see the point and besides Juno gets annoyed if my anger calls him and he's got no one to bite. What you did is in the past, it's over. Believe or not, I spent a lot of my time while I was kidnapped ranting about your behavior and dreaming about how I was going to kick your ass if I saw you again. It kept me going when I wanted to give up. There was no way I was going to die without making sure you knew what you were missing first. What's brought this on? Is this about Raff and how you used to treat him?"

Nereus, Raff, and Teilo left an hour earlier, tired and happy. It'd been a day full of laughter and jokes and Sebastian loved the closeness his best friend shared with his mates. All Nereus ever wanted was to be loved and he'd found it with his wolves. Sebastian was stunned Raff talked Nereus into seeing his second father, Abraxas, and they were all friends now too. Nereus held his grudge against Abraxas longer than Sebastian had with his father. It'd been a good day and yet, when Madison had gone for his shower, rather than follow him, Sebastian found himself dwelling on the past instead.

"It's got nothing to do with Raff, although I'm pleased Dad and the Fates dealt with the bastard who took you and Raff," Sebastian said in a low voice. "But don't you understand, I'm the guilty one. I should be suffering under Hade's torture as well. Nereus met Raff the same day I met you; he was thrilled. I was a bastard. I bet he's never caused Raff an ounce of hurt, or Teilo either. But I hurt you; with my words, my lack of action. You were kidnapped because of me; you stayed kidnapped because of me. I don't know how you can forgive me."

"Anger wouldn't have achieved anything and I think deep down I always knew you needed love in your life," Madison said simply. "I'm not going to lie and say there weren't some rough moments, but when I actually got the chance to talk to you, when I realized you weren't just playing with my emotions, I didn't see the point in dwelling on the negative stuff. You are who you are, and if I ever had the opportunity to meet this Alexander of yours, I'd probably thank him for showing you what love and loyalty were all about."

Sebastian's mouth dropped open. "You wouldn't."

"Meh, no, probably not," Madison grinned. "But then you wouldn't have a lot of positive things to say to my father, who, by kicking me out of his pack allowed me to come here, build a life for myself and eventually meet you. They're in the past, can't you see that, and what I can say about Alexander, from all I've read about him, is that if we ever did meet, he'd be the first one to congratulate me on being with you. Wouldn't he?"

Sebastian thought back on the memories he had with his ex-lover and nodded. "Yeah, he would. He was a good man like that and he always wanted me to be happy."

"Then that's how I want you to remember him," Madison said softly. "As a good man with a lover to call his own. Now please, put that knife away. I hate seeing something so freaking expensive just stuck in the wall."

My mate, ever the practical one, Sebastian smiled as he got up and retrieved the knife. "You reckon a museum would want this?"

"Of course, it's a piece of history. But," Madison shook his head. "Love, you don't have to give it away. I don't feel threatened by a piece of hardware, no matter how pretty it is."

"It's all I have left of him," Sebastian said, hefting the knife in his hand. It felt solid, dependable, but Sebastian preferred his knives with a lot less glitter. Something Alexander had never considered. It was his turn to shake his head. "I really don't think we need it cluttering up our space anymore, do you?"

"If you're sure," Madison said, his blue eyes warm with the love Sebastian knew he had for him. "Now put it away and come to bed. You can talk about Alexander if you want to, and I won't get mad. Or...." He eased his towel from around his waist.

"We can make more memories of our own," Sebastian grinned. Madison's open arms let him know he'd made the right decision.

The End...but read on, as an added bonus in this book I've included the story of Thanatos and Cody. I am sure you're curious about them ☺

Always Enough

Thanatos and Cody

Chapter One

Cody came close to dropping his tray as he saw a man appear in the middle of the club; he just materialized out of nowhere with Madison by his side. Madison, who'd been kidnapped and was being held naked in a cage according to the gossip was now sporting an expensive suit and a jeweled tie. His wolf snarled at the easy way the gorgeous man rested his hand on Madison's shoulder with such familiarity and his wolf's reaction made Cody sniff, almost instinctively, and then wish he hadn't. There, through the scents of all the others rushing to greet them, he smelled it. Cinnamon and apple pie. The smell of home. His eyes filled with tears and slipping his tray onto the nearest table, he scurried out of the room.

There's only one man in existence who would remind him of the life he'd been stolen from years before. But Cody knew he couldn't have a mate. He'd never be worthy of a being like the man who commanded so much attention by simply appearing. And there was no denying the man was his mate. His wolf howled at him to go back and fight Madison for his place by the man's side.

Running to his room, Cody slammed and bolted the door, even as he berated himself for his childishness. The man must have magic to appear like he did, but he wasn't a shifter. He wouldn't have scented him. He didn't even know Cody existed. "But now I know about him. I've seen him; I've scented him. I will never be able to get close to anyone ever again."

Cody sat on his bed, tears streaming from his eyes as he faced the empty bed Joel left behind. "I don't know what to do," he whispered as he had countless nights when his friend was there.

"I can't be a mate, you know what we went through. He's not going to want me when he hears my story. You know that. I know that. What should I do?"

Of course, Joel didn't answer. Joel was buried on pack grounds after his life had been cut short by a madman. A madman Cody could have gone with that night but didn't because Joel pleaded with him for a chance to secure a permanent master.

"It's not fair," he whispered. "Life just isn't fair." Memories inspired by his mate's scent flooded his brain. His mom baking in the kitchen; his dad, a familiar presence at the table reading the paper once he got home from work. His twin sisters, Sarah and Clare would be playing in the corner. Cody squeezed his eyes tight. He'd been taken two weeks before his eleventh birthday. Stolen by a charming wolf who told him he was taking him to see his mom at the store, as he wandered home from school.

"I was such a fool," Cody shook his head. In the early days of his captivity, he used to dream about his father storming in to save him, but within a few months, those dreams passed, like the other childish dreams he had about his life. Cody learned the best way to avoid a fist was to do as he was told and keep his feelings to himself. As the years passed, he kept his head down, accepted he had no control over his body and followed every order he was given. His crowning achievement was being introduced to Damien and being accepted on his fuck-roster. Jacob had been thrilled and made plans about what Cody was expected to do when he became Alpha Mate.

Of course, that didn't happen. Damien didn't even know his

name, preferring to call him and the other subs on the roster "boy," and then, of course, Scott came along – Damien's true mate. Cody found he didn't mind his time on the roster. He wasn't expected to subject himself to the demands of anyone else and he got three good meals a day and a shared room at the back of the club. Damien was never cruel; he just never noticed who was sent in to service him. He was too busy doing important things like being the alpha and keeping the club safe for the pack.

It was Madison who chose him for the roster, Cody remembered, and his wolf growled in his head at the mere thought of the name. Madison was a good wolf who didn't let his position as PA turn him into a snob. Cody always enjoyed his company. Gossip around the club claimed Madison found his mate just before he'd been taken; a mate who didn't want him. *Maybe he can have mine, they look good together*, Cody thought although his heart dropped like a stone at the very idea.

I'm going to have to leave. I can't stay here and run the risk of that sexy man recognizing our bond. Unfortunately, while Cody knew exactly who could get him out of his current predicament, he hesitated to pull out his phone. *He won't want me if I've been crying, I'll send him a message tomorrow,* he thought, remembering the human's insistence on a lack of noise or response during their scenes. It was almost as though he wanted a pliant, silent toy, but Cody could handle that.

Only Joel ever knew Cody slipped out of the club to meet the man he called Master K. Damien didn't allow humans in the BDSM side of his club, but Cody met the man while working the bar. The hundred dollar tips and Joel's urgings were enough to convince him to meet the man in a human club more than once, although he hadn't seen Master K in over two weeks. Master K had a collar for him and at the time Cody wasn't sure if he could make that commitment because it would mean he'd have to leave the pack. Some of Master K's other conditions also made him think twice, and yet he knew the offer was still open. The daily texts reminded him of that. *At least he won't expect me to have sex;* surprisingly enough that was Master K's hard limit. No sexual contact of any kind.

In any other circumstance, Cody would have talked to Madison about Master K – got some advice and reassurance Damien would take him back in the pack if he left for a while. But Cody couldn't talk to him this time. He had to make the decision on his own and as tears continued to roll down his cheeks, he accepted he had no choice. He would miss the club, running as a wolf, playing with his friends. *I'll miss my mate too,* Cody thought sadly as he curled up on his bed. Deciding he'd pack first thing in the morning, he buried himself under his blankets and cried himself to sleep.

Chapter Two

Thanatos let himself into the room once inhabited by Joel and Cody, shutting the door behind him. Closing his eyes, he allowed his senses to pick up the emotional energies left in the space. It was easy to pick out which was Joel's bed. The last time the boy had been in the room, he'd been excited and happy. Keeping his eyes closed, Thanatos watched as Joel was talking to his best friend, thanking him for the chance to be with Larson. That this could be his big break in finding someone permanent to care for him. Thanatos shook his head sadly. He'd seen too often when a need for affection drove someone to go against their gut instincts. But at least the energies in this room were positive ones and Thanatos knew the Fates would make good on their promise Joel's next life would be a happier one.

His eyes still closed Thanatos tuned into Cody's energies. The man wasn't there, of course. In fact, none of his personal possessions were in the room anymore. The energies were strong; pain, despair, heartbreak and Thanatos quickly opened his eyes as his mind was filled with the image of his mate crying on his bed. "You haven't left me a lot to find, young Cody," he said softly as his eyes scanned the room. Two single beds neatly made; two dressers with nothing on top of them. There was a small table with a television resting on it, the dust marks showing that pictures used to sit on top of it, but had been moved. There were no pictures on the wall, no personal possessions at all.

Moving to the dresser closest to Cody's bed, Thanatos opened the top drawer. He was surprised to find an envelope in there, addressed to Madison. Knowing Madison was probably changing his clothes for the tenth time since he left him getting ready for his date, Thanatos slit it open and pulled out the single sheet of paper.

Hey Mads,

Don't look for me, okay? I know Damien will be pissed I left without telling him, but I've got an offer. The chance to be collared. I know the guy is human, but he will take care of my needs. He's promised that at least. I'm sure I'll be fine and you guys won't need to worry about me anymore.

I don't know how much of the gossip is true, you know what the club is like, but I'd heard your mate was stupid enough to turn you down. What an ass. You've always deserved someone who'd treat you special. Let him know what he's missing. If anyone can make him pay for his mistakes, it's you.

I'm so glad you're safe, but that guy you came home with, well don't tell him, but he's my mate. You have to promise me, Mads. You know why I can't be with him. I'm too broken and damaged to have a fine-looking man like that in my life. If he knew the truth about me, he'd run a million miles in the opposite direction and who could blame him. But don't let him, okay. I saw that fancy tie you were wearing and the snazzy suit. If your mate won't come to the party, then take mine. He'd be proud to have you by his side and I know you'd look after him for me. Make him happy, please.

Love you Mads.

Cody.

"Oh, Cody, you are truly a treasure among wolves," Thanatos smiled through his tears. "As if I'd run from someone with a heart as big as yours." He ran his hand over the paper. "Show me where he is." The paper glistened, went translucent and Thanatos growled at what he saw. Crumpling the paper into his pocket, he waved his hand and disappeared from the room.

/~/~/~/~/

Cody shivered with cold, his hair falling over his face as he tried to find the calm center that protected his psyche from harm. He knew he'd made a mistake as soon as he'd arrived at the texted address. He was running late because the taxi driver wasn't familiar with the richer part of town and while Cody's hopes rose when he saw the solid nature of the family home, they were dashed within a minute of arrival. Master K grabbed him roughly by the arm and hustled him through the house so fast he didn't have a chance to admire the soft furnishings or the elegant pictures on the wall. Instead, he'd been pushed through a hidden door in the back of the pantry; his bag snatched from his shoulder as he was shunted down into a basement room with nothing but a large chest and a spanking bench to break the gloom.

"Get undressed," Master K said roughly. "You were supposed to be here twenty minutes ago."

"The taxi..." Cody started to explain, but he was roughly cut off.

"I don't want excuses. I have a meeting. Now get your clothes off."

"If you show me where you expect me to stay, then I can organize my belongings and be prepared for you when you get back." There was no sign of a bed or bathroom facilities in the dank room, and Cody wanted to shower.

"I said get undressed. You don't give the orders around here, I do." Master K raised his fist and Cody quickly disrobed, his wolf screaming at him they were in danger. His clothes were wrenched from his hands and stuffed into his bag; his old school backpack which was the only thing he had left from when he'd been stolen from his home.

"Get on the bench, I can't have you roaming around while I have company."

"I think I made a mistake," Cody said with more courage than he felt. "Give me my clothes, I want to leave now."

"You're not going anywhere," Master K said cruelly. "This room is soundproofed, there's only one door and I have the key. Now get on that bench."

Cody debated his options for all of two seconds. His wolf was clamoring to get out and even in his human form, he could easily overcome his new Master. But then Master K said in a jeering tone reminiscent of his past, "No one knows you're here. No one in that

341

fancy club is going to miss a *nobody* like you and as you said this morning, I'm all you've got left. Where are you going to go, if you leave here? It's no fun being homeless. Now, I won't warn you again. Get on that bench."

A nobody, that's all I've ever been. He's right. No one's going to miss me and I've got nowhere left to go. With a sinking heart, Cody arranged himself over the bench and didn't make a sound as Master K strapped him down and left him under the glaring lights, taking his bag and clothes with him.

Chapter Three

Thanatos lingered in the walls, his powers allowing him to remain invisible unless he chose to reveal himself. The basement room was squalid, cold and dirty. Cody was strapped naked to a spanking bench; his lightly tanned skin glowing under the stark fluorescent lights, highlighting the goosebumps. It was torture for Thanatos to see his mate exposed in such a way, but he willed himself to bide his time. He needed to see for himself who Cody trusted enough to run to. Somehow, from the energies infesting the concrete walls, Thanatos didn't think Cody found the savior he was seeking.

He didn't have long to wait. The battered wooden door opened silently and an average looking human stepped into the room. Thanatos quirked his eyebrow. With all the strong Doms in the club, this is who Cody thought would keep him safe? He ran his eyes over the man wearing what looked like coveralls. Cody's master was about five foot ten, thinning mousy brown hair and small dark eyes. The darkness in the man's aura worried Thanatos. Black spots, like the ones he could see, indicated this man was spiraling into the dark side. He didn't like the way the human's eyes gleamed at the sight of Cody on the bench either.

"You haven't tried to get away. What a good boy." The man's mocking tone made Thanatos cringe, but Cody didn't move. There was no reaction or sound to indicate he even knew the man was there and Thanatos tensed. Had he done the wrong thing by leaving Cody tied up? Only the shallow rise and fall around Cody's ribs and his skin tones indicated he was alive at all.

"Your silence pleases me," the man said. "You were always one of the better ones. I have to wonder at your training, given how you just accept anything I dish out." Thanatos felt a chill running down his spine as the man grabbed Cody by the hair, pulling his head up.

"You wanted a collar from me, isn't that right? You can answer."

"If it pleases you, Master." Thanatos closed his eyes briefly. Cody's voice was devoid of emotion and he had to wonder how far Cody sank into his mind to escape his situation.

"Collars are earned by good boys who deserve them, aren't they? Answer."

"Yes, Master."

"Have you earned one, boy?"

Cody's mouth opened and then he shut it again. The man laughed. "Oh, you are good. My perfect little toy." He dropped Cody's hair and ran his hand down that slender back; Cody never moved. It was Thanatos who fisted his hands. He didn't know exactly how long Cody had been confined but his muscles must have been screaming. He made to step out from the wall, but the man's voice stopped him.

"You won't be missed, Cody. So many young boys like you, all craving the security they'd been told comes from having a collar. But you boys are all the same. Greedy, conniving, manipulative. You think to lure someone with your blond curls and your big blue eyes. *Take care of me master.* Just like all the others. You make it so easy. As if you think a hot ass is going to give you rights to my paycheck. I hate you all!" He slapped Cody's butt hard, leaving a clear imprint.

Cody stayed silent but his shoulder's slumped. Thanatos

could see his eyes were closed and it was as if he was blindly accepting his fate. Fortunately, Thanatos wasn't as accommodating. He slipped from the wall, pulling on his Death persona like a cloak.

"Take your hands off that boy," he said, his deep voice booming around the concrete blocks.

The human choked and stepped back. "Who the hell are you? This is my home. How did you get in here?"

Thanatos threw back his hood, knowing all the human would see was the skull the world recognized as representing the Grim Reaper. "I thought my looks made it obvious. I'm Death and I have a soul to collect." He glanced down at Cody. His mate wasn't afraid. In fact, there was a tinge of hope in his aura.

He was shocked when the human laughed. "You're about thirty minutes too early. I haven't finished with this one yet. But you can hang around if you want to watch. I'm sure you must get off on this sort of thing."

Thanatos's surprise grew. Was this human so steeped in his own depravity he'd forgotten what it was like to feel fear?

"It's not his soul I've come to collect," Thanatos said, letting his voice deepen further. "This young man has a bright future filled with love, laughter and anything his heart desires. Yours, however. Your time is up."

"No!" The man frantically grabbed his heart, his gut and then his head. "I went to the doctor last week. He said I was in perfect health."

"He can't see the state of your soul," Thanatos intoned. He felt the familiar tingle on the back of his neck and knew the Fates approved what he was about to do. "Every time you take the life of an innocent a large black stain sullies your soul. Those spots are growing." He stepped closer until he was standing by Cody's side. The human staggered against the wall, his face sweating, and clutching his chest. "They get so big they crush the light you were born with, stealing your breath." The man started to pant and then he choked and gasped, his mouth working frantically trying to draw in air.

"The pressure causes your heart to pound erratically; it can't cope with the strain. You're being crushed by the darkness – the darkness you created with every life you stole. With no light to ease your heart's way…." Thanatos paused as the human let out a cry and fell to the floor, his hand still clutching his shirt. "Your heart stops. You die."

He watched dispassionately as the man's soul left his body and slid through the floor. Hades could play with that one. He turned to see Cody watching him, hope and awe warring in his expressive eyes. "Hey, little one, are you comfortable with me getting you out of those shackles?"

"Please," Cody's voice was soft. "I made a stupid mistake and I'm sorry to have caused any bother."

"We all make mistakes, sweetheart," Thanatos grinned as he waved his hands and the shackles fell away from Cody's wrists and ankles. "Would you like some clothes?" He asked as he helped Cody sit upright on the bench.

"My stuff," Cody looked around the room. "He took it. I don't have much but...."

"Hold my hand," Thanatos noticed he was still skeletal but Cody didn't hesitate. Thanatos was aware of heat and cursed his lack of nerve endings. "Now think of your bag and click your fingers...with your other hand."

Cody chuckled. It wasn't much, but Thanatos felt a warmth he hadn't felt since Sebastian was born. "There you go," he beamed, as the battered backpack appeared in Cody's hand.

"My stuff," Cody shook his head, a smile on his lovely face. "It's all I have in the world. I know it doesn't look like much, but it means everything to me. How can I thank you?"

"By agreeing to have dinner with me?" Thanatos suggested. "Oh, not looking like this," with a wave of his hand he changed into his mortal persona; definitely more suitable for dinner dates.

Cody's mouth dropped open. "It is you. I wondered...I thought...my wolf said...but we couldn't scent you...you saved me." Thanatos found himself with an armful of naked Cody and while that was doing all sorts of things to parts of him that remained dormant for decades, he wanted his mate to know their relationship would be more than sex.

Although it seemed Cody already knew that because there was nothing sexual about the way he rubbed his face on his shirt. Sensual definitely, but it was almost as though the young shifter was looking for comfort; something Thanatos was happy to provide. Wolves thrived on touch, he remembered, and as he held Cody close and lightly stroked the blond curls resting on his chest, he made sure his hips were angled away.

"I know you won't keep me after you learn my story," Cody said, pulling back after a long moment. "I understand and won't stop you from walking away. But thank you for saving me. For coming after me. No one has ever looked out for me like that before. I'll never forget your kindness."

Thanatos couldn't resist stroking Cody's cheek, so glad he had flesh this time and could appreciate the softness. "I already know your story," he said softly, doing his best to ignore Cody's look of abject horror. "You've had a rough life and if you ever want to talk about it, I will hold you close and let you talk as much as you like. But don't ever think I'm going to reject you because of it. You don't know me yet, but when you do, you'll realize I'm not that shallow."

"Oh no, I didn't mean, I'm sorry. I never meant that...."

"I know," Thanatos said. "Now, I don't know about you, but I could do with a hearty meal. How does Paris sound?"

"Paris, Texas? But we could eat at the club if you wanted to. I get my meals for free." Oh, what a thoughtful and sincere look on such a handsome, sweet face. Thanatos wanted to give Cody the world.

"Paris, France, my sweetheart," he corrected gently. "I know a lovely little café that's open late. Now why don't you put some clothes on, or I can dress you if you prefer."

"Like you did Madison?" Cody laughed as he pulled away from Thanatos and hunted through his bag. "I'd be too scared of wearing anything that expensive – imagine spilling sauce on that tie; you'd never be able to clear the stain away from the jewels." He held up a pair of black pants and a white tee-shirt, both horribly crumpled. "I don't want to look a complete wreck, though. Is there anything you can do with these?"

Burn them? Thanatos smiled and flicked a finger leaving Cody dressed in stylish black jeans, a crisp pale blue button-down shirt that brought out the color in his eyes and a pair of gleaming black leather boots. "That wasn't exactly what I meant, but thank you." Cody smiled again looking down at his clothes and running his hand over the shirt. Watching him, Thanatos became aware of another problem; his leather pants were exceptionally irritating around a persistent erection.

Unwilling to change in front of Cody and thereby drawing attention to his rather large concern, Thanatos tucked his mate under his arm and closed his eyes. "Hold on tight," he said as he snapped his fingers.

Chapter Four

Cody felt like he'd fallen down the proverbial rabbit hole. Less than twenty-four hours ago, he'd been crying in his bed, grieving a mate he knew would never care for him, and now, here he was in *France* listening to his mate order their food like a native. At least, he guessed that's what his mate was doing. The cute waiter seemed to understand him and was smiling and waving his arms a lot.

"I am sorry," his mate said when the waiter finally sashayed away with a wink and a smile. "I come here often, but this is the first time I've brought a date. Juan was curious about you."

Cody appreciated his mate explaining but he had something more important on his mind. "I don't know what to call you," he whispered, looking around. There was only one other couple in the small restaurant and they were holding hands and staring into each other's eyes.

"I have many names, but socially most people call me Thanatos. You don't want to hear what some of them call me when I'm on the job." Thanatos chuckled, revealing perfect white teeth.

"Thanatos," Cody tried the name on his tongue. He liked it. It seemed to fit his mate who looked as though he'd be at home either in a gym or a business meeting. Thanatos didn't have the long hair shifters favored; instead, his almost black hair was short around the sides and back, with a mop of curls artfully tousled on top. His face was squared until his jaw line that curved into a strong triangle. There was a hint of a dimple covered by a well-groomed beard, trimmed to enhance his jawline and mouth. Combined with full lips, a long straight nose and eyes that focused on his like lasers, Cody gripped the napkin on his lap to stop from groaning.

"Like what you see?" Thanatos's grin turned his face from CEO stern to drop-dead drool worthy.

Oops, probably shouldn't use that expression around him. Cody almost giggled but managed to stop himself in time. Truth be told, he wasn't sure if he was dreaming or not. An attentive date, dining in a totally different country; after the shock of his morning, he was feeling lightheaded. "I'm sure you're aware of how striking you look," he said, reaching for his glass. "I'm equally sure you could have anyone you wanted with a simple snap of your fingers."

"So could you," Thanatos said with an easy smile, "and all that means is that we make a stunning couple. Juan certainly thought so."

Cody could see why some people might think that. He was fair,

Thanatos was dark. His frame was a good six inches shorter than Thanatos's and Thanatos's shoulders were almost twice the size of his. "Can you tell me about yourself?" he asked, "or is that not allowed."

"I'll answer any questions you have," Thanatos said, "but some of the answers might require more privacy than this."

Just then the waiter returned with two steaming plates and Cody felt his stomach rumble appreciatively. He peered at the plate cautiously, sniffing as soon as the waiter went away.

"It's okay," Thanatos leaned towards him. "I wouldn't order something you'd never had before, not on our first date. This is beef bourguignon. The meat is cooked in red wine with onions, mushrooms, a hint of garlic and bacon pieces."

"Smells delicious," Cody said, although he waited until Thanatos picked up his fork before he started eating.

Unfortunately, no matter how wonderful the food tasted or how charming Thanatos was being, telling him the highlights of Paris history, Cody found it difficult to focus and when the plates were cleared away he just had to ask. "Why Madison? I love the guy, don't get me wrong, but why save Madison and not Joel? They were both captured by the same man."

A frown flickered so quickly over Thanatos's face, Cody almost missed it, but his mate nodded as if expecting the question and beckoned to Juan for the check. "That is something best discussed at home, sweetheart. Shall we get desserts to go?"

/~/~/~/~/

Thanatos always intended to be honest with his mate if he was ever granted one, but his meal wasn't sitting comfortably as he transported them both to his home in the Underworld. He closed his eyes briefly and willed his section of the house warded for security and privacy before managing a smile. "I can make coffee or we can have more wine. Do you want these desserts now, or shall I put them in the refrigerator?"

"Coffee, if it's not too much trouble and yes, I'd like to wait for dessert. Shifters can't get drunk, but I'm feeling a bit lightheaded. It was a lovely meal, thank you."

Cody wasn't as relaxed as he'd been in the restaurant and Thanatos's fears were confirmed when the young man asked, "Is it just you who lives here, or do you share this place with others?"

You promised honesty, Thanatos thought. Aloud he said, "I'm the only one here at the moment, but I offered Madison a room when I saved him and Sebastian comes and goes as well. But this section of the house is my private wing and completely secure." Cody tensed at the mention of Madison's name and Thanatos quickly flicked up a tray with all the things needed for coffee and led his mate through into his small private sitting room.

"You have a lot of things," Cody said, but unlike other rare visitors he didn't immediately go over and start touching the array of objects Thanatos had on his shelves.

"I've lived a very long time." Thanatos put the tray on the coffee table and sat on the leather couch. "Sit sweetness, it might take me a little while to answer your questions. The concepts of life and death aren't easy."

Cody perched on the end of the couch and Thanatos warned himself that was better than choosing a single chair. He poured the coffee while thinking about what to say. Handing Cody his cup he said softly, "I am truly sorry about Joel. Madison told me he was your closest friend. Please know I shepherded his soul to the afterlife personally and the Fates have assured me he will be reborn and his life threads will be much happier in the next life. He will find his mate and be happy for a very long time."

"But why didn't that happen this time?" Cody said, his brow sporting a cute furrow. "Joel never hurt anybody. He was stolen from his family just like I was, but when he tried to find them again he found out they'd all perished in a car accident. He was only twenty-one, but he had so much life and he was a good friend. He just wanted to be accepted for who he was and now he'll never have a chance. It doesn't seem fair."

Thanatos sighed. This was why he never got close to anyone who knew who he was. "Not in this lifetime, no, but it's been promised in the next, you have my word. Do you believe the Fates weave the threads of life?"

"Sort of." Cody was still frowning and Thanatos racked his brains trying to think of a way to describe the Fates role in life.

"Imagine life as one huge tapestry, a brilliant picture with every color of the rainbow flowing across the weave."

Cody nodded.

"This picture has shades of light and dark so that every strand is highlighted in its own way. It's the Fates's job to see to it the picture always stays balanced. If there's too much of one color, then the individual strands aren't appreciated for their own beauty. If there is too much dark, then the picture is spoiled. The Fates work tirelessly to keep that balance."

"So, you're saying Joel's thread was too bright and was cut short?"

"Sort of," Thanatos nodded encouragingly. "The length of a person's thread is determined the moment it is woven into the tapestry. Some are short, some are long and some, like mine, are part of the structure of the weave and can never be cut."

Thanatos waited for his mate to ask about the length of his own thread, but Cody surprised him. "Does that mean you saved Madison because it wasn't time for his thread to be cut? I mean, I can understand why you would, because as Death you can't let people die who aren't supposed to otherwise the picture is unbalanced. But you said he lives here with you. Do you offer your home to everyone whose life you save? If so, you must have a wicked big house."

Chuckling, Thanatos shook his head. "Madison is a special case, he's my son's mate. The Fates made him a part of the weave when Sebastian refused to accept him. He's immortal now, no matter what that son of mine does."

"You have a son? He refused Mads? What's wrong with him? Oh shit. Sorry. He's your son." Cody studied his fingers on his lap. "Do you have a wife too? I guess you must have if you have a son."

"I had a wife," Thanatos said sadly. "She died when Sebastian was born more than five millennia ago."

"She died, but you...." Cody's eyes widened and then he slipped off the arm of the couch and Thanatos felt strong arms around his neck. "How horrible for you," he whispered and Thanatos knew Cody meant it. Closing his eyes

367

Thanatos took the comfort offered, holding his arms loosely around Cody's waist.

"You don't have any say in how long a person lives?" Cody asked. It was Thanatos's turn to shake his head. "So, when the time comes and my thread ends, you'll have to take me to wherever it is I end up?"

"No, precious," Thanatos said softly. "The Fates aren't cruel. Pragmatic sometimes, but never cruel. You were born to be my mate. Whether you accept me as a mate or not, you will always be part of the weave, the very foundation of the tapestry, just like Madison."

"Are you sure the Fates know what they're doing? Because I have to tell you, Mads can be a handful sometimes." Then Cody quickly clapped his hand over his mouth, his eyes wide as he looked over his shoulder.

"It's okay," Thanatos smiled. "We all have days when we wonder what the Fates are doing."

"But they can hear us, right? See us?" Cody's eyes scanned the room as if expecting a shadowy figure to be standing there.

"No. Well, they could if they wanted to," Thanatos agreed, "but I've worked for them since life began. They'll make sure we're not disturbed for at least a week to give us a chance to get to know each other."

"You said you already know me," Cody's gaze came back to him, his eyes searching as though memorizing his face.

"I know your pain, sweet Cody," Thanatos agreed, "but there's a lot more to you than how you responded to what life has thrown at you. It's the same with anyone. Often our pain is the only thing we can feel, but underneath that, our

369

spirit has the power to do great things; and we've seen that in history – people using their pain to build wonderful lives for themselves and for others around them. You have that potential and I think with support and encouragement you can fulfill it."

"I didn't even get to go to high school," Cody said with a sigh, his eyes apparently examining Thanatos's chest. He tried not to puff it out because what Cody was saying was important but he was conscious he wasn't as buff as some of the wolf shifters he'd seen.

"I was only eleven when I was taken," Cody continued. "I'm not clever, or good at talking about world affairs or anything. I can cook and do chores but I'm afraid, after seeing you in that restaurant, you're going to find me terribly dull. I don't know any other language but English and I've only ever seen the places you've talked about in books."

"Do you like reading?" Thanatos had an idea.

"When I get a chance to go to the library," Cody nodded. "They have these amazing big coffee-table books in there about every country in the world. The pictures are so vibrant and I would spend a lot of my downtime poring over them, learning as much as I could about other places. Before that, I only had one book. It was left in my backpack – I was supposed to return it to the school library that day, but I forgot. I don't know why Jacob let me keep it, but I was so glad. It was the only book I was allowed to touch for years until I mentioned it to Mads one day after Jacob was killed and he took me to the library and helped me get a card and everything."

Thanatos found Cody's honesty and lack of self-pity surprising and really sexy. "I have a huge library you can read anytime, but I was thinking, later, you and I can visit these places so you can see them with your own eyes. Would you like that?"

Cody's eyes widened with excitement. "It would be a dream come true, especially with you by my side. It's not as though we'd have to worry about plane travel," Cody said softly, hooking his arms around Thanatos's neck. "But tell me sweet Death, with you so powerful, strong and able to click anything you want in life; what can someone like me do for you?"

"Give me a safe place to fall," Thanatos said honestly. "A reason to come home, someone who will smile at me instead of looking at me with horror or sadness and who will give me a hug when I have a bad day." Thanatos was taking a risk, laying all his hopes and dreams on his mate on the day they'd met, but he'd waited so long for someone who could simply be there for him he found he couldn't keep quiet. He held his breath, praying for a positive answer.

Cody let out a soft breath and then smiled as he nodded. "I think I can do that. In fact, for you, I know I can."

Chapter Five

Cody couldn't explain it, but hearing Thanatos be so open with him settled him in a way he couldn't describe. He would have laughed if told the personification of Death was a person who needed a hug at the end of a rough day. The idea as a concept was ludicrous. And yet, being curled up in Thanatos's arms, hearing his heart beat, feeling the soft rise and fall of the man's chest – it made his mate appear more human. And while human wasn't something Thanatos would ever be, Cody had never felt closer to anyone in his life.

Which raised a very human/shifter problem. Thanatos's scent was driving his wolf wild and his cock crazy, and given his current position, it wasn't something he could hide from his mate for long. He didn't want to hide it, but he hesitated...he'd never been allowed to be forward with anyone.

"You know, I've always believed clear, concise communication is the key to successful relationships," Thanatos broke into his thoughts. "When my dear Myra was alive she used to scold me for not being more open with her and I've strived to do better ever since. I know there's something worrying you, but unless you tell me, I can't fix it."

Cody shook his head with a grin. Of course, Death figured he could fix anything; in most cases, he probably could. "It's part of my being broken, I'm afraid," he said, knowing he'd never lie to his mate. "I've been trained for a long time to behave in a certain way and yet this time, here with you, I find myself struggling – what I want and what I might be allowed to do."

Thanatos's lip quirked on one side. "In other words, we're talking about sex."

Cody blushed and nodded.

"I know you're aroused," Thanatos's grin widened. "It turns your aura into a beautiful shade of purple."

"I can smell you want me," Cody offered shyly. It seems they could communicate in some ways better than others.

"And yet we're at a stalemate; sitting like two respectable nuns at a charity event." Thanatos paused for a moment and then said, "If I tell you why I haven't stripped you naked yet, will you explain to me why you haven't wrestled me down and claimed me?"

Cody was so shocked he laughed. "I wouldn't do that to you. I couldn't. You're so much bigger and stronger than I am."

"And yet, I would submit gracefully if I knew that's what you wanted."

Cody's heart raced at the thought. "It is, at least that's what my wolf wants, but I've never…."

"Others in your life have always taken the lead," Thanatos kindly finished for him. "And you see, that's the key element of my dilemma. I want you madly, badly, passionately…."

"And yet because of what I've been through in my past, you hesitate because you don't want to hurt me or for me to think you're using me like other's have done." Cody thought for a moment. The situation was definitely awkward; the smell of arousal filled the air as though their conversation had given Thanatos license to let his true feelings show. Cody's need increased and was bordering on painful.

"I think," he said slowly, meeting Thanatos's heated gaze, "we should think about meeting in the middle."

Thanatos raised an eyebrow. "I'm not quite sure what you mean."

"I mean," Cody drew on every ounce of confidence he had, "we should start with a kiss and let nature take its course. We both appear to want this claiming to happen." He leaned forward slightly.

"She's a wonderful lady, Mother Nature, I must take you to meet her one day," Thanatos said as he leaned closer too. "You are so beautiful, Cody, so perfect in every way. I want to claim you as mine with every fiber of my being."

Cody wasn't sure about the perfect comment, he knew he wasn't. But as he and Thanatos inched closer and closer together, he knew it wasn't the time to debate the concept. His mate agreed to a claiming. He wanted to be claimed. Thanatos's lips were right there, slightly moist, full and Cody ached to taste them. One slight push of his body and they were touching, lips to lips, Thanatos's chest lightly grazing his. Cody tilted his head as their noses bumped and Thanatos took his gesture as the invitation it was. Moaning, Cody closed his eyes and sank into his first real kiss. It was just as heavenly as the books described.

/~/~/~/~/

Thanatos fought to keep his desires in check as his tongue caressed the inside of Cody's mouth. He wasn't a shifter; he wasn't ruled by instincts or strong desires. Poseidon called him boring more than once and even Hades considered him too gentlemanly to ever have any real fun. But he wasn't feeling very gentlemanly with Cody in his arms. He felt savage, primal and the word *Mine* was beating a jungle rhythm in his head. Cody was sweet, succulent and fit so perfectly in his arms, Thanatos's head swam as the blood in his body migrated south.

Take it fucking slow, he warned himself even as his hand mysteriously found its way under Cody's shirt. The heat from Cody's skin burned his fingertips and before he knew it both hands were memorizing the light definition of Cody's back muscles and the sweet swell of his ass.

"Mmm, you taste scrumptious," Cody whispered against his cheek. Thanatos shivered as a shy tongue traced the edge of his ear and as Cody's throat was right there, he took advantage. At the first brush of his lips against pale flesh, Cody arched his neck and Thanatos groaned. He nuzzled the flesh, nipping and kissing his way from ear to ear.

A hot hand grazed over his pectoral muscles and Thanatos grinned against Cody's neck as he realized his mate was taking some initiative. At least half of his shirt buttons were undone. Tentatively at first, Cody's explorations grew bolder and while Thanatos could easily magic away his clothes with a thought, he cautioned himself against it. Cody would learn they had an equal partnership, but trust took time to build. Thanatos wasn't going to do anything to jeopardize that simply because of a strangled cock and a need he didn't totally understand.

Instead, he gently nudged at Cody's shirt, willing it away. Cody took that moment to suck his earlobe and their chests met, flesh on flesh. Cody seemed to have developed extra hands, and everywhere the frantic wolf touched Thanatos's skin tingled. He needed them on a flat surface. His cock was squeezed in the folds of his suit pants and weighted down with Cody's body, it had nowhere to go. Hoping he wasn't pushing things too fast, Thanatos closed his eyes and with a wish, they were flat on his bed.

"Took you long enough." Cody grinned as he shimmied down Thanatos's body and attacked his zipper. Attacked was the only word he could use. The light graze of claws tickled his abdomen and the sounds of ripping cloth hit the air. Having never bedded a shifter, Thanatos stilled, unsure if he wanted sharp bits near his junk. But all those doubts disappeared as his cock barely had time to stretch in relief before it was enveloped in moist heat.

"Fucking hell," he groaned, as his head hit the mattress with a thump. Working out how long it'd been since he'd felt the warmth of someone's mouth around his cock required too much brain power and

Thanatos didn't have any to spare. He wasn't small; men and women alike balked at seeing him naked. But Cody had no reservations, swallowing him down, his full lips stretched wide. Thanatos raised his head to look and then slammed his head back down again. His hips twitched with the need to thrust and Cody encouraged it, bobbing his head up and down, Thanatos's cockhead grazing the back of Cody's throat with every down stroke.

"I'm going to come," Thanatos yelled as a tingle tickled his balls. Instead of pulling off, Cody's head bobbed faster, and as two claws lightly grazed over the taut skin of Thanatos's scrotum, Thanatos groaned to the heavens as his balls emptied.

Dizzy with the afterglow, his endorphins racing around his body, Thanatos waved his hand. "Come up here," he moaned, his arms pulling his mate close as Cody moved up the bed. "I'll return the favor in a minute."

"I'm hoping you'll do more than that," Cody whispered against his lips and as strong hands wound around his neck and fingers gripped his hair, Thanatos groaned at the taste of his spunk mixed in Cody's saliva.

"Will you bite me if I take you?" He asked when they both came up for air. Cody's hair was a mass of curls, his blue eyes sparkled against the red of his cheeks and his lips were like two red marshmallows.

"Are you worried if it will hurt?" Cody asked, a cute frown leaving lines on his forehead. "Because, from what I've heard it only hurts for a second and then usually you get a massive orgasm from it."

"I'm not worried about the pain, sweet one. I'm asking if your wolf, if *you* want to claim me."

"Of course, I do," Cody protested hotly. "It's just if I do, you'll never be able to get hard for anyone else." His voice trailed to a whisper at the end.

"I know about that," Thanatos said, rubbing his thumb along Cody's mouth. "I'm aware of how wolf shifters are with mates, and I love that you'll never have to doubt me because I get called away with my job. Will you wear my mark, right here?" He stroked down the side of Cody's throat. "I want everyone to see it." His voice dropped and his cock perked up at the idea of Cody wearing the Grim Reaper's scythe along his throat. No one would be able to doubt his pretty wolf was mated.

"We both love that idea." Cody blushed. "Did you want me to get on my hands and knees now, because my cock is about to fall off?"

Thanatos waved his hand and the rest of Cody's clothes fell away. He knew without checking, his mate would already be well-prepped and lubed. Power had its advantages. "I want to see your face when I make you mine for eternity," he said huskily as he rolled Cody onto his back, looming above him.

/~/~/~/~/

Cody parted his legs quickly, eager to feel Thanatos's weight on top of him. He resisted a squeak when his ass was suddenly elevated with a pillow and he bit his lip as he felt the unmistakable nudge of Thanatos's cock against his hole. Inhaling deeply, he slowly blew out a long breath, willing his body to relax as Thanatos thrust inside. To his surprise, there was no pain, no tearing of skin, just an ache in his groin which was nothing more than his cock demanding attention. He glared at Thanatos's hand. "Did you?" He clicked his fingers.

"Just this once." Thanatos lowered his body over his and Cody felt his skin tingle everywhere their skin met. "I understand prepping can be enjoyable foreplay, but I'd far rather spend time kissing you instead."

Making a mental note to let his mate know he could do both at the same time, Cody wrapped his arms around Thanatos's long neck and closed his eyes. In his encounters in the past, closing his eyes was Cody's way of escaping a sometimes unpleasant situation. He would focus his mind on his happy place and stay there until the deed was done.

But there was no need for escapism this time. This time he was savoring Thanatos's scent, the slight grunts the man made every time he bottomed out. Thanatos's lips were sensual, masterful and even a little playful, and where balls met butt cheeks, Thanatos's hips kept up a rhythmic thrust designed to tease and torment, keeping every one of Cody's nerves alive. He was full, deliciously full and it took Thanatos only a few strokes to find his hot spot. But rather than punch at it like a rabid bull, Thanatos kept things sensually slow as though they had all the time in the world.

Only Thanatos's eyes signaled the passion he was controlling. When kissing had to stop because neither man could breathe, Cody felt a gentle finger against the side of his eye. "See me," Thanatos whispered, and somehow Cody knew this was important to his mate. Opening his eyes, he stared into the depths of Thanatos's soul. He saw the need Thanatos had for him, the love he believed was already there but most of all he saw the giant heart his mate had to hide because of his position among the gods. He'd spent just a wretched ten years hating his life; Thanatos had carried his burden for millennia.

"I'm yours," he said softly, hoping Thanatos would read the depth of the message behind those simple words. "Mark me for eternity."

Thanatos's eyes widened for just a second and then Cody felt a branding hand on his throat as his mate tilted his head back and called to the heavens. "Hear me Fates, for I am Death, your ever-obedient servant. Gift my mate with all he'll need to rule the Underworld by my side. Record it in the heavens, I am Thanatos and I will be CLAIMED."

The last word was roared and Cody felt a surge of energy flood his body. His hair crackled, his skin was on fire and he shut his eyes against the bright red glow that flooded their room. Thanatos roared again as his hip thrusts stuttered and then he shoved his cock deep inside and stopped. "Bite me," Thanatos's words were guttural as he leaned down.

Cody opened his eyes and saw the visage of the Grim Reaper lurking under the skin. *If I'm dying this is a hell of a way to go,* he thought as he felt his teeth drop and his wolf leap forward. He pulled Thanatos down and sank his teeth into his mate's flesh; his wolf howling in his mind as he bit as deep as he could, his cock pulsing between them. Thanatos's blood coated his tongue and he felt a foreign presence in his mind. He smiled and carefully withdrew his teeth, licking over the wound which was already healing. Thanatos stayed slumped over him and Cody realized the extra warmth he was sensing in his ass area was the evidence of his mate's release. He was so caught up in the idea he'd claimed his mate, he'd totally forgotten about that side of things. Pressing his lips together to stop from chuckling, Cody let his eyelids fall and enjoyed the comforting weight of his mate's body on his.

"I'll never give you cause to regret this," Thanatos promised, his breath wafting through Cody's hair.

"I'm going to spend eternity looking after you; I'm so glad we found each other," Cody said with a smile. He opened his eyes. His wolf had calmed down, was preening at claiming such an important mate. But Cody could still hear howling. "What's that noise?" He asked, looking across at the window. The bright red of before settled into a gentle glow, but Cody couldn't see anything else.

"Juno and the rest of his hellhounds," Thanatos muttered. "Welcoming you and your wolf to the Underworld. They'll shut up in a minute."

Hellhounds? Cody wondered as his eyelids started to close. He was vaguely aware of Thanatos waving his hand again and as he drifted off to sleep, clean and curled up safe in his mate's arms, the eerie howling was almost soothing.

Chapter Six

Cody wandered around Thanatos's huge mansion, sighing as he inspected the massive paintings on the walls. He was bored. The pictures were clearly originals, as were the historic knickknacks Thanatos arranged on shelves all over the house. The red carpet was thick and warm under his feet, and the high cream ceilings didn't have a mark on them. *Dusting would be a full-time job on its own,* he thought, but of course, there was no one employed to do any of the housework. Given that this was Death's domain, Thanatos controlled everything with one negligent wave of his hand. Dust didn't stand a chance.

I could go back to the library, but Cody was there earlier that morning. After their five-day "holiday" Thanatos had to go back to work, something he was loathe to do, but Cody understood.

Thanatos explained he didn't attend every death in the world; that would be impossible. He attended special cases; violent deaths where the soul wasn't ready to leave the earthly plane; children who had no one waiting for them on the other side and natural deaths where the person might be hesitant wondering if their loved ones would be waiting for them. He pushed, he encouraged and sometimes even tore souls from their bodies, depending on the situation.

Just the night before Thanatos had come home pale and shaking after dealing with a young man whose soul was already black. It seemed even the strongest of bad guys got scared when faced with death and this particular man didn't want to go to the torment he sensed was waiting for him in the afterlife. He put up a huge fight, one that Thanatos could have won easily if he hadn't been so shocked at how young the soul was.

A warm bath, a back rub, a hug and a smile went a long way towards helping Thanatos feel better, but while he was away, Cody found he had nothing to do. Thanatos's kindly, "you can do anything you want so long as you don't go outside," was well-meaning and thoughtful, but not a lot of help. Cody was used to working all day and half the night. There was nothing needed doing in the mansion.

Determined to be more proactive, Cody turned and headed for the kitchen. Yes, Thanatos could create food with a wave of his hand, but there was no reason he had to. Cody had always wanted to spend time in the club kitchens, but Boris was never keen on letting anyone into his domain. Thanatos's kitchen was huge and had every appliance known to man. Cody knew it was well stocked, not only because Madison and Sebastian shared the house, but because Thanatos was worried he wouldn't eat while he was off doing his job.

Wondering how his friend was getting on, Cody was shocked to see Madison sitting on the kitchen counter eating a huge sandwich. "Hi, there," Madison said, smiling around his sandwich. "I see you've finally come up for air. I tried to visit, but Dad's warded his rooms so me and Sebastian can't get in."

Cody blushed. He knew exactly why Thanatos didn't want his son or his son's mate in his rooms. It seemed his mate had let his libido lapse for years, unwilling to engage in hookups he may have to collect a soul from, but since his mating, he was making up for lost time. He didn't have any exhibitionist tendencies either, much to Cody's relief.

"Yeah, Thanatos is doing his protective bit right now. I'm sure it will ease off over time. How're things with Sebastian? I haven't met him yet."

"He wants to meet you," Madison winked. "I've been teasing him for days about having a new stepfather."

"Stepfather?" Cody squeaked. He knew about Sebastian, obviously. Thanatos loved his son with a passion even if Sebastian didn't seem too keen on their relationship. "But he's older than you and me put together. He doesn't need another parent."

"Doesn't mean he doesn't have one," Madison said cheerily. He stuffed the last of his sandwich in his mouth and chewed quickly. "So, are you here for food, or just learning your way around?"

"Bored." Cody wandered over to see if there was anything in the fridge. He could eat a sandwich, but he'd be eating just to have something to do.

"We could let our wolves have a run," Madison hopped off the counter. "I promised Juno I would pop out and say hi."

Cody twirled so quickly he almost tripped over his own feet. "You run with the hellhounds? Thanatos said I wasn't allowed outside the building."

Madison huffed. "He's being an overprotective ninny. The hellhounds are the enforcers of the Underworld and I just might have been made their Alpha after killing a rogue and claiming Sebastian." He polished his nails against the edge of his jacket and winked at Cody.

"You are?" Cody squealed and ran over, giving Madison a big hug. "I'm so freaking proud of you." He grinned. "I bet that put Damien's nose out of joint."

"Yeah, he banished me there for a while, said I could be a danger to the pack because of my new position." Madison frowned.

"Oh Mads, how awful for you." Cody hadn't even considered his pack position. He hadn't been back since he'd been claimed.

Madison waved his hand. "Pff, it's all good now. Got a new title, Chief Operating Officer, a salary increase and days off – all things I didn't have before and Sebastian is running the club with me, so things couldn't be better."

"Where is Sebastian?" Cody looked around. "Did you two have an argument or something?"

"Nah, nothing like that," Madison laughed. "I wore him out. He's still asleep. Come on, let's go for that run."

Cody glanced out at the barren landscape, still glowing red through the kitchen window. "Thanatos won't be very happy with me," he said quietly.

Madison slung his arm across Cody's shoulder. "I bet you haven't had an argument yet, have you?"

Cody shook his head. "Thanatos is really good to me. We haven't had any reason to fight."

Madison sighed. "Then you haven't had the chance to feel the joy of make-up sex either. You're missing out."

Cody eyed his friend warily. "What's so great about make-up sex compared to any other kind." He thought he and Thanatos were doing perfectly fine in that department.

"It's hard to explain," Madison said staring out the window. "More passionate, primal; when

Sebastian is pissed off with me, he's amazing in the sack."

"And he isn't any other time?"

Madison slapped him on the arm. "Of course, he's fucking amazing, but I don't want him to hear me say that. He has a big enough ego as it is. Now come on. You're mated to the ruler of the Underworld; well, one of them anyway. No one has explained what Hades does around here, but don't worry about it. We have the hellhounds for protection and I can talk to Juno through some wacky mind link, so you'll be fine. You should spend time outside. You're looking peaky."

"I am not peaky," Cody snapped back. But he allowed Madison to drag him out of the kitchen and through a utility room where Madison found a hanger and slipped off his suit jacket, hanging it carefully.

"Come on, get your gear off. You can't shift like that," Madison said. "I've got to move fast before Sebastian wakes up."

"You mean he doesn't want you going outside either?" Cody tugged at his shirt and jeans as he slipped off his boots. "Then why are we doing this?"

"Sebastian isn't silly enough to stop me going outside, but he would insist on coming along. Won't it be more fun, running with others on four legs?"

Cody nodded as he began his shift. He didn't have a problem being naked around others but since he'd been claimed it felt a bit strange. The tattoo on his neck seemed to heat up as he called his wolf and somehow the process seemed to go faster than normal and as he shook out his fur he still felt a bit strange.

"Holy fucking shit, look at the size of you." Madison's eyes were almost popping out of his head and Cody looked across and realized he was almost as tall as Madison...who was still on two feet. He looked down and then looked around. His shoulders were a lot taller than the washing machine.

Crap, what's happened to me? He turned, trying to see the rest of his body. His coloring was still the same, but his chest was bigger and his tail was a lot longer than he remembered.

"I was going to suggest we use the doggy door," Madison pointed to the hatch in the door. "But I don't think you'd fit."

Cody whined and slumped on the floor. There wasn't a lot of room and Madison almost fell over his back leg. "It's not a bad thing," Madison said softly, stepping over the offending limb and stroking Cody's ears. "There are some nasties out there although the hellhounds will keep us safe. I wonder why you got the size, though, but I was made the Alpha?"

Cody thought back to his claiming night where he felt he'd been changed on a molecular level. It would seem his long legs were one of the gifts the Fates thought he needed to rule by Thanatos's side, although he couldn't think why. He'd never been a fighter and he couldn't see that changing.

Naked, Madison opened the door and then released his own wolf form. Now he was shifted, Cody could see the differences between them clearly. On past pack runs, his brown and red wolf form was the same size as Madison's white one; now Madison's head barely reached his shoulder with his neck stretched out.

With an encouraging bark, Madison trotted out of the mansion heading straight for the edge of the lawn. Cody followed cautiously, looking around at the land he now called home. At first glance, there was nothing to recommend it. The slightly undulating landscape was red, broken only by black twisted trees and the odd ramshackle building that looked like one stiff breeze would knock it down. Even the sky had a reddish glow. Thanatos's white mansion and bright green lawn stood out in stark contrast.

On the edge of the large grass area, seven huge dogs stood silently waiting. The hellhounds were all black, *surprise, surprise*, and sported flatter faces than the wolves, although their teeth were long and gleamed white against their fur. As Madison approached, they all bowed their head and then to Cody's shock they bowed to him as well.

You honor us with your presence, Mate of Thanatos, a voice said in his head.

Thank you, Cody sent back, or at least he hoped he did. He wondered if he should incline his head, but his wolf didn't think it was a good idea. He looked across at Madison. Even in wolf form, his friend looked like he ruled the world. He was so tiny in comparison to the dogs, but they all moved out of his way when Madison pushed through them.

It looks like the Prince wishes to go for a run, the courtly voice came through again. *You may run with me if you like.* Scanning the hounds, Cody saw one, in particular, watching him. Moving forward, the same dog fell into step beside him and they took off across the landscape, the hounds howled as they ran.

Chapter Seven

Thanatos shimmered into his apartment and immediately looked around for Cody. His quarters felt empty and as Thanatos closed his eyes and scanned for the whereabouts of Cody's soul, he quickly learned why. "He's left the house," he muttered, as he stormed out of his apartment and through to his son's side of the house.

"Sebastian! Sebastian!" He pounded on the door.

"Where's Madison?" He growled when a tousled, half-naked Sebastian finally opened the door.

"Fuck, I don't know," Sebastian rubbed his hand over his face. "Probably in the kitchen, knowing him. He's always eating. I don't know where he puts it all."

"Come with me," Thanatos grabbed his son by the arm and frog marched him down to the empty kitchen. "Any other bright ideas?" He asked waving his hand.

Sebastian frowned and looked around. Then he rushed into the utility room. "Fuck!" He yelled as he saw the discarded clothing. "I told him not to go without me."

"You let Madison run with the hounds?" Thanatos snarled.

"I can't stop him, he's their Alpha now. Juno said he had to run with them once in a while. It makes the hounds feel important or some shit, I don't know. But he knows damn well he's not supposed to go without me." Sebastian ran his hands through his hair and then clicked his fingers – his sweat pants giving way to his usual black shirt and camo pants and most importantly, boots.

"I told Cody he wasn't supposed to go out at all," Thanatos said angrily, "and I can only assume your precious Madison talked him into it."

"Or maybe, your mate has a mind of his own and knows how to use it," Sebastian said, thumping the washing machine. "I wouldn't know because you've kept him locked up for well over a freaking week and I haven't met him yet. I can imagine how hard that might be on him, sitting around by himself while you're working; considering he's wolf and used to being around others all the time. Shit, I know Madison's tried to see him a number of times and can't get through the wards you set up. No wonder he ran off. He's a wolf shifter and you've locked him in a fancy cage!"

"No!" Thanatos stumbled back against the wall, horrified at the very idea. "I wouldn't do that...I just wanted...oh, fuck no." He covered his face with his hands. "What the hell have I done?"

Sebastian's hand was strong on his shoulder. "You're simply doing what any of us do with a true mate – trying to protect him. But Madison thrives at the club, he needed to be part of the pack and when Damien threw him out he was devastated."

"Damien threw Madison out?" *Fuck,* Thanatos thought, *I need to keep on top of things.*

"He did and then he begged and groveled to get Madison back. We both work together there now. But have you asked your mate about his pack position?" Sebastian sauntered over to the back door.

"I didn't think he had one," Thanatos said, remembering how he and his little mate met. "I thought he left the pack. I don't know. Cody's talked about traveling, and...shit. I don't know."

"Er...if that's your mate running with Juno and the others, then I'm not sure you want to mention pack position. Damien's likely to shit a cow when he sees a wolf that size." Thanatos hurried to where Sebastian was peering out. Coming over the distant hills he could make out Madison's white form immediately and the seven hounds were all familiar to him.

"Oops," he said as he watched the unfamiliar wolf running and leaping over the hounds, apparently having a great time. "I think the Fates might have got a bit overzealous when I asked them to bless him with the powers he needed to rule with me here. I'm fairly sure he wasn't that size before."

"He wouldn't have been or he'd be the Alpha of the San Antonio pack. I'll ask Madison if your mate's powers have increased when he's in his human form. That's what caused the problem for him. As soon as he went to the club, everyone knew something was different about him. Malacai snitched, Damien got shitty because Madison stamped his foot and the hounds appeared on the pack grounds and I spent five days with a crying mate in my arms."

"I'm more curious about any other powers he might have," Thanatos said thoughtfully. "If I knew he was better able to protect himself, then maybe he could go to the club with you and Madison sometimes. Or do you still have a twink problem?"

Sebastian laughed. "You honestly think Madison would let me get away with that attitude? It's no fun sleeping on the couch. Nah, if Madison says it's okay, I won't have a problem with Cody coming with us. Madison tells me he's a good man, your new mate."

Thanatos's heart warmed. His son had finally grown up. He'd always been proud of Sebastian and was crushed by their split so many centuries ago; although he knew at the time the Fates were right and he'd done the right thing. The only concession he'd got from the Fates was that Alexander and Bagoas would always be reincarnated on a different continent to wherever Sebastian happened to be. He knew the mated couple wouldn't recognize his son, but he'd never understood the true depths of Sebastian's powers and didn't want to take the risk.

"Let's hope Cody's powers are the more muted kind then," he said. "I guess we're about to find out." He stepped out of the door as Madison and Cody loped across the lawn, both of their tongues hanging out. Madison jumped straight into Sebastian's open arms, his tongue slathering Sebastian's face. Thanatos watched as Cody seemed to hang back, his exuberant, free-spirited mood from seconds before subdued as he hunched his shoulders and slunk forward, his tail down.

"Did you have fun, sweet one?" Thanatos asked, making sure he had a friendly smile on his face as he covered the distance between them in a blink of an eye. Cody tilted his head and Thanatos's mind was filled with images of running, jumping and playing with the hounds. His grin widened. "Thank you for sharing that with me. Looks like you had a great time."

Cody's tail started to wag slowly. "I'm not angry with you," Thanatos ran his hand over Cody's solid head. "Worried about you, that comes with being mates, but I'm the one who should apologize here." Cody looked puzzled and Thanatos was seized with a sudden need for his mate's human form. "I was just thinking, we've never explored the gifts the Fates blessed you with. I can see your wolf form has grown. Can you try shifting with your clothes on?"

Cody's head tilted the other way and then he shimmered and stood on two feet, fully clothed. "I did it. This is so cool."

His smile was Thanatos's undoing. He crushed Cody against his chest and smashed his mouth over those ruby red lips. Cody moaned and clutched at his shirt apparently just as desperate to get closer. It was only a loud and extremely fake cough that stopped Thanatos from stripping his mate bare and plowing into him on the lawn. He pulled his lips away reluctantly and glared at his son.

"Not that you two don't look super-hot together," Sebastian said with a smirk, "But Madison reminded me shifters like to eat after a run. Do you want to join us for dinner?"

What a day for surprises, Thanatos thought as he looked down at his mate. Cody nodded his approval although he seemed to prefer using Thanatos's bulk to hide from

Sebastian. That wouldn't do. Especially when their dinner was the first time Sebastian had offered to share a table with him in longer than he could remember.

"Come and meet our son," he said softly, ignoring Cody's surprised stare. "Sebastian, this is Cody, my true mate."

"And, according to Madison, my new stepfather," Sebastian grinned as he held out his hand. Cody went to take it, but then Sebastian grabbed his wrist and pulled him closer. Within seconds, Cody was back in Thanatos's arms and Sebastian was sprawled on the ground, ten feet away.

"What the fuck?" Sebastian grumbled as he pushed himself off the grass. "I was only going to hug him."

"It wasn't me," Thanatos said shaking his head at his bewildered mate.

"I don't know what happened," Cody whispered. "I hugged Madison earlier and nothing went wrong. I'm so sorry," he added in a louder voice to Sebastian.

"No problem Pops, we'll try it again, gentler this time." Thanatos watched as Sebastian gingerly got closer and wrapped his arms around Cody's slender frame, keeping the hug short and perfunctory. It was still more than Thanatos expected. "Welcome to the family," Sebastian said, releasing him quickly. "You don't mind if I call you Pops, do you?"

"Er...no," Cody still looked bewildered, but then he grinned. "So long as you don't whine at me for your allowance every week or expect me to change your stinky diapers."

"Oh, I think your mate and I are going to get along just fine. Let's go get something to eat," Sebastian said with a laugh as

Madison came out to join them, clothed this time.

Thanatos followed his sons back into the house, his mate tucked under his arm. In the evening that followed he sent a quiet word of thanks to the Fates. His house rang with the sounds of laughter, the air filled with the delicious smells of a meal shared. With Cody sitting proud and happy by his side, and Sebastian smiling in his direction every time he said something, it was all more than he'd ever hoped for. His house was finally a home.

The End

Of course, with me, it's never really the end. This new series will explore the adventures of some familiar faces, linked to but not actually members of the Cloverleah Pack. But don't despair, there will be regular appearances by members of my favorite pack. The next book in this series will be Poseidon's story. You met him in *On the Brink* and so many people have written to me and asked if I could find him his own mate. I did. Look for that book sometime in May.

Other Books By Lisa Oliver

Cloverleah Pack

Book 1 – The Reluctant Wolf – Kane and Shawn

Book 2 – The Runaway Cat – Griff and Diablo

Book 3 – When No Doesn't Cut It – Damien and Scott

Book 3.5 – Never Go Back – Scott and Damien's Trip and a free story about Malacai and Elijah

Book 4 – Calming the Enforcer – Troy and Anton

Book 5 – Getting Close to the Omega – Dean and Matthew

Book 6 – Fae for All – Jax, Aelfric and Fafnir (M/M/M)

Book 7 – Watching Out for Fangs – Josh and Vadim

Book 8 – Tangling with Bears – Tobias, Luke and Kurt (M/M/M)

Book 9 – Angel in Black Leather – Adair and Vassago

Book 9.5 – Scenes from Cloverleah – four short stories featuring the men we've come to love

Book 10 – On The Brink – Teilo, Raff and Nereus (M/M/M)

Book 11 – (as yet untitled) – Marius and (shush, it's a secret) (Coming April 2017)

The God's Made Me Do It (Cloverleah spin off series)

Get Over It – Madison and Sebastian's story (you just read it)

Bound and Bonded Series

Book One – Don't Touch – Levi and Steel

Book Two – Topping the Dom – Pearson and Dante

Book Three – Total Submission – Kyle and Teric

Book Four – Fighting Fangs – Ace and Devin

Book Five – No Mate of Mine – Roger and Cam

Book Six – Undesirable Mate – Phillip and Kellen

Stockton Wolves Series

Book One – Get off My Case – Shane and Dimitri

Book Two – Copping a Lot of Sin – Ben, Sin and Gabriel (M/M/M)

Book Three – Mace's Awakening – Mace and Roan

Book Four – Don't Bite – Trent and Alexi

Book Five – (as yet untitled) – Captain Reynolds and Nico (Coming March 2017)

Alpha and Omega Series

Book One – The Biker's Omega – Marly and Trent

Book Two – Dance Around the Cop – Zander and Terry

Book 2.5 – Change of Plans - Q and Sully – short story, (Coming soon)

Book Three – The Artist and His Alpha – Caden and Sean

Book Four – Harder in Heels – Ronan and Asaph

The Portrain Pack and Coven

The Power of the Bite – Dax and Zane

The Fangs Between Us – Broz and Van – a Portrain Coven and Pack Prequel (coming soon).

Balance – Angels and Demons

The Viper's Heart – Raziel and Botis

Passion Punched King – Anael and Zagan – coming March 2017

Shifter's Uprising Series – in conjunction with Thomas J. Oliver

Book One – Uncaged – Carlin and Lucas

Book Two – Fly Free (Coming soon)

And under my Pen Name, Lee Oliver

Northern States Pack

Book One – Ranger's End Game – Ranger and Aiden

Book Two – Cam's Promise (late March 2017)

About the Author

Lisa Oliver had been writing non-fiction books for years when visions of half dressed, buff men started invading her dreams. Unable to resist the lure of her stories, Lisa decided to switch to fiction books, and now stories about her men clamor to get out from under her fingertips.

When Lisa is not writing, she is usually reading with a cup of tea always at hand. Her grown children and grandchildren sometimes try and pry her away from the computer and have found that the best way to do it, is to promise her chocolate. Lisa will do anything for chocolate.

Lisa loves to hear from her readers and other writers. You can friend her on Facebook (http://www.facebook.com/lisaoliverauthor), catch up on what's happening at her blog (http://www.supernaturalsmut.com) or email her directly at yoursintuitively@gmail.com.

Lisa also writes similar, shorter books under the pen name Lee Oliver.

Made in the USA
Monee, IL
19 May 2020